CASS TELL

DANCE WITH POETIC SEA

A Novel

destinēe

Contents

To see a world in a grain of sand,
And a heaven in a wild flower,
Hold infinity in the palm of your hand
And eternity in an hour.
William Blake

To know wisdom and instruction,
To understand the words of the wise.
From The Book of Proverbs

Footprint 1: Know your stage and the part you are playing.

All the world's a stage,
And all the men and women merely players;
They have their exits and their entrances,
And one man in his time plays many parts.
William Shakespeare

Saturday

I t was a muggy August day, and I sat on a park bench, staring at the ground, daydreaming. I had not been well over the past months, and that's where I went to think.

While lost in my introspection, a man with black leather shoes approached me, and asked, "Why are you sitting here?"

It was an odd question and caught me by surprise. "What?" I responded, looking up at him.

"You shouldn't be here." He spoke with an Eastern European accent.

"Why not?" I demanded, feeling annoyed, thinking the guy was abnormal. You get strange people in Central Park.

The man wore jeans, a black suit jacket, and a dark blue shirt. His black hair was combed straight back, accentuating his broad face. Sweat drops were on his forehead. My instinct was to ignore him and go back to my soul-searching.

"Why are you here?", he asked.

His question was a distraction, and I should have connected the dots. There had been a series of brutal beatings of homeless people in Central Park. One died. It was a gang of young thugs having perverse fun. But, this guy wasn't that young, maybe forty years old.

He gave me a hard stare, thereby diverting my attention from a rustling sound in the leaves behind me. I turned and was shocked to see another man swinging a baseball bat at me. He was a left-handed batter. A second later the bat cracked against my head, and stars exploded. I fell to the ground, rough asphalt digging into my hands and knees. The bat struck my shoulder, and the man with the black shoes kicked me in the ribs and grunted, "Goodbye, Mack."

Then there were more hard kicks. I tried to roll up in a ball to avoid the beating, as pain rippled through my body.

In the distance, I heard a female voice scream, and the two men stopped. There was another hard blow to the side of my head, and then there were choppy sounds as the men ran away. I tried to rise but fell back to the ground, struggling to stay conscious.

It was a secluded place in the park back in the trees, and if anyone saw me laying there, it wasn't evident. Or, maybe they didn't care? Walk on. Don't get involved. Or, perhaps the woman who screamed ran away in fear.

My eyes slowly opened, and the world was a hazy carousel. I took a deep breath and then pushed up from the ground and plopped onto the bench.

Gradually, my senses came back, and I assessed my condition. I was wearing shorts, and both knees had red scrapes. There was a tear in the old t-shirt I'd been wearing for a week or more. With a painful movement, I raised my hand and touched my six-month beard where blood dripped down from a cut on the side of my head.

In university, I was a linebacker on our football team and had taken hard hits. The pain from this attack was worse than anything experienced on the football field.

I reached into the back pocket of my shorts and took out my wallet. My cash was still there, close to six hundred dollars. Were the men there to rob me, or did they have a different purpose?

The cut on the side of my head continued to bleed, and I regretted they had stopped the beating. One or two more blows from the bat and they could have broken my neck. Little did they realize that I might have paid them to do so.

* * *

Time ticked by as I sat on the bench. I felt nauseous and wanted to vomit, so I took a couple of deep breaths. Blood dripped from my beard to the front of my t-shirt. Someone had left part of a newspaper on the bench, the weekend business section. I took a page, folded it several times, and held it to the side of my head.

My body throbbed with pain, and it was difficult to breathe. A rib felt broken. Maybe this was a sign. Things had not gone well over the past six months and this only added to my misery. I wondered if I had the strength to get back to my apartment. Did it even matter?

I sat in silence, hopeful that a few minutes of rest would give me strength. Glancing at the newspaper, I noticed an article with a strange title. It said, ''Poetry for Business: The Lost Component of the Manager's Soul'' That was weird, but at that moment so was the entire world.

When attempting to stand up, the dizziness returned, so I sat down, and my eyes went back to the newspaper article. It was about some bizarre thing where the marketing team from a large corporation went on a one-week workshop to write poetry.

My immediate reaction was that corporations had gone lunatic, doing such strange things as meditation seminars, and team building exercises of rock climbing and floating down rivers in rafts. But, poetry? What better way to waste shareholders' money? My head throbbed with pain.

I quickly skimmed the article, not in any condition to read it word for word. The marketing team claimed the workshop had opened new ways to see the world. It helped the team members become more creative and released them from constraints.

Poetry for business was beyond weird. I remembered that someone once wrote, "Poetry is like truth. Most people are not interested." But, one word in the article jumped out at me, the word *constraints*. Indeed, over the past months, that word applied to me. That word flashed with each throb in my head.

Then, I saw a policeman approaching me. Perhaps the woman who screamed had informed him. When he got close, he asked, "What happened?"

"Two guys blindsided me."

"Did you see them?"

"Briefly, but then the lights went out. It was a baseball bat." They didn't play for the New York Yankees.

"Can you give a description?"

"One was around forty, heavy built, black hair combed straight back, a white guy. He wore a dark suit jacket and black leather shoes. I can't describe the other one. Maybe if I saw him again, I'd recognize him."

"Forty?"

"Something like that. The man had an Eastern European accent."

"That's strange. There have been attacks in the park, but it was younger guys, a vigilante group intimidating helpless people. And, they did use bats."

He didn't say homeless, as though he didn't want to offend me.

"You don't look good," he said. "I'll call an ambulance, and we can get you to a hospital.

"It's okay. I think I can walk. I'll go to the Medical Clinic." There was one about a block away.

"Are you sure?"

"I think so," I said.

I stood up, wobbled a bit, and then we walked together to the medical clinic, the policeman holding my arm. Luckily the clinic wasn't busy, so right away they took me to a room, and a doctor sewed seven stitches along my hairline. He then covered it with a bandage.

After performing an examination, the doctor said I had a concussion. He gave me painkillers and anti-inflammation pills. His advice was to lay still for a couple of days. Removal of the stitches could be in seven or eight days.

Another policeman showed up, and he took photos. After they made a report of my description of the attack, the two policemen left the clinic.

Then I went back to my apartment, and it felt like the past hour was just a small part of a long, depressing nightmare.

* * *

In my kitchen, I got a glass of water and slowly drank it. I didn't know what felt worse, my head, shoulder, or ribs. The scrapes on my knees were secondary. Slowly I gathered my senses. When looking down at my knees, I noticed the page of the newspaper sticking out of my pocket.

I took it out and put it on the table, and again the title of the article caught my attention. So, I sat down and read it, this time in more detail.

It said that a university professor, Dr. Rachel Eden, taught a poetry workshop. She had written a new book titled, *The Mystery of Wisdom,* and the subtitle was, *Seeing through the eyes of a poet.* The premise of the book was that people in our Western culture had lost the ability to discern. Poetry was a way of enabling this by finding new perspectives and releasing from constraints. Again, the word *constraints* jumped out at me.

Her course was not specifically about writing poetry. It was more about thinking like a poet, at least in seeing in a new way. Her seminar was for teachers and creative types, but also for business teams.

I was anything but a creative type, living my days surrounded by numbers and flowcharts and technical indicators. My days were mechanical and calculated. Poetry was the farthest thing from my normal existence. I was a stock trader.

Dr. Eden gave her workshops at a hotel in Spain, so I figured that the cost of the marketing team to get there had been considerable. I knew the company they worked for, having analyzed their financials. It was no wonder their profits were in the pits.

The *constraints* word continued to pound in my head. That word was relevant. During the past months, I had become a boat without a rudder, without a sense of purpose. To avoid self-destructing, I retreated into a cave, and then life became restricted.

The article triggered my curiosity. I made my way to my office, went to my computer and did a search for more information on this workshop. I found Dr. Eden's website and quickly read through the home page. Then, I went to the contact page and saw a telephone number.

A flash went through me. It was like making a spontaneous trade. Most of the time, I made an exhaustive analysis before buying or selling a stock. Although, there were occasions when I went on instinct or feeling, immediately pushing the buy or sell button.

On an impulse, I picked up the telephone and made a long-distance call to Spain.

It was difficult to see through my swollen left eye, so it took several tries to get the telephone number correct. I spoke with someone for a few minutes, made a decision, and then gave my credit card number. When the call ended, I went back to my computer and booked a first-class air ticket.

After removing my shorts and torn bloody t-shirt, I took a shower, the first one in many days. I did my best to keep the bandage on my forehead dry. Shaving my tender swollen face was impossible, but I managed to trim off much of my beard. I didn't attempt to give myself a haircut.

I placed band-aids on the wounds on my knees and put on clean jeans and a new blue t-shirt. Not knowing what clothing to take, I packed a medium-sized backpack with a summer jacket, a pair of shorts, a couple of t-shirts, socks and a few other basics. I figured I could buy anything I needed once arriving at my destination.

I found my passport, put a laptop and smartphone into a computer bag, turned off my computer, and left the apartment.

Several hours later, I was on a flight to Barcelona. Once up in the air something occurred to me. How did those thugs in the park know my name?

* * *

On the all-nighter flight, I tried to sleep, but every position was painful no matter which way I shifted my body.

It reminded me of my football days, where one played through all kinds of physical pain. The first-class seat should have made me comfortable, but it didn't work. Drinks were served, and I wondered if alcohol would help. Is it okay to consume alcohol if you have a concussion? Should you even be on an airplane?

The flight attendants served the meal, but I declined, as my stomach was queasy. Instead, I took the painkillers given by the doctor.

One of the attendants brought me ice in a cotton towel, and that eased the aching on my swollen eye, so I rested my head and tried to relax.

I thought back to the morning which had started with my usual routine.

The alarm had gone off at five, and I got out of bed, went over to the curtains and opened them. It had been a gray morning with August humidity hanging in the air. That didn't matter because most of the time I stayed in my air-conditioned apartment.

After putting on my well-worn shorts and a dirty t-shirt, I walked barefoot into the living room and looked through the large windows at New York City skyscrapers. My apartment is twenty floors up, containing four large bedrooms and four bathrooms, plus an office. For months the doors to three of the bedrooms had been closed. I only used my bedroom, the office, and the kitchen.

The living room, which I rarely went into, is massive, furnished with large couches. We purchased the apartment a year ago because Linette liked it. Except for my office furniture, she bought everything, the sofas covered in soft leather, comfortable beds, luxury tableware, and every other kind of classy furnishing. She purchased a range of high-end electronic equipment for blending, juicing and baking, although much of the time we ate out. Expensive paintings were on the walls in all the rooms.

That morning, which was exactly like every other day, I made coffee in the kitchen and then went to my office. My computer ran non-stop, feeding data to four large monitors. The stock markets were still open in Asia and Europe. We were in the world of twenty-four-hour trading, seven days a week. There was always something to buy and sell.

I sat at my desk and strategized my trades, and then the U.S. markets opened, and I was in business. There are a million ways to trade, whether in stocks, bonds, futures, or options. I specialize in one method, value trading. Simply defined, value investing is when you select stocks that trade for less than their intrinsic value.

That was the strategy I perfected when managing my mutual fund. There is little subjectivity in my methodology. Fundamentally it's a step by step procedure that suits my temperament, though lately, it felt too mechanical. In fact, everything in my life felt that way. It was like being imprisoned by a twenty-four hour a day routine, like slow-walking on a never-ending treadmill.

My typical day consisted of watching computer screens, even when working out with the weights and elliptical trainer set up in one corner of the office. The freezer was full of ready-made dinners ordered online. The coffee machine and the microwave were the two main appliances used in the kitchen.

Occasionally, I went out to sit on the bench in the park, like this morning, or was it yesterday morning because of the time and date change depending on where my flight was over the Atlantic? The first two hours of trading were successful, and my portfolio rose by seventy thousand dollars. My account had grown over the past six months, with a total value in the millions. The zeros were meaningless. It was nothing more than an online game, and I was addicted to it.

I didn't like to go out, because down the street from my apartment is the financial district, full of banks and investment companies. I spent ten years down there, first starting out as a junior trader, but was quickly promoted to manage a mutual fund.

During those years, I lived a financial manager's lifestyle, with the stress of the markets during the day, and after meeting Linette, the evenings and weekends became filled with social life and making connections. Linette loved parties. She became a member of the elite in New York City, and my money enabled her to maintain her lifestyle.

Linette had cupboards full of clothing designed by the exclusive names in the fashion industry, and she looked outstanding in everything she wore.

Her looks gave her power, and with one alluring glance, you were captured by her hypnotic spell.

During that time, I became acquainted with influential people, many of them holding significant positions in my mutual fund, but six months ago, I walked out of my company and lost contact with most of them. I still communicate with my lawyer, Ben Akerman.

I can honestly say that I dislike New York City, but I don't have the incentive to move anywhere else. Burnout and depression destroy one's motivation.

I sometimes thought about the guys working in those buildings, how they are caught up in life routines driven by the pressures of the stock markets. I wouldn't go back to that no matter what they offered.

Personally, those buildings represent a hurt, and it is difficult to shake it off. That's why I hide behind my computer screens. I probably should see a shrink, but is it worth it?

I can't cast judgment on those people, many putting the god of money first in their lives. For me, the money isn't primary. As one trader put it, "it's just a way of keeping score." In my case, a routine controlled me. Get up, play the markets, workout, eat and drink, and go to bed. It's a pattern repeated each day, again and again.

The question is, why am I addicted to this mechanical, repressive way of living? When I consider people on Wall Street, it's like they are acting out parts in a play. I once read, **know your stage and the part you are playing.** My stage had now become very small and restricted, nothing more than a room with a computer. My part was to enact an endless series of meaningless repetitions. If that's the role I should be playing, then life was dreadfully limited.

Maybe the world is not a stage. It is more like a game, and I have mastered a tiny piece of it. Whether it's a stage or a game, I questioned if I was bringing anything beneficial to anyone in the world? The honest answer was no.

Being unable to sleep during the flight, every half hour I stood up, although it was impossible to stretch my body because of the pain. Perhaps I overdid it with the painkillers, and I finally dozed off just as they started to serve breakfast, about an hour and a half before landing. Once the plane was on the ground and the passengers were leaving, the flight attendant had difficulty awakening me.

When I walked off the plane and into the Barcelona terminal, bright sunlight struck my eyes through the large glass windows. I could now see through a small slit in my left eye. A line of people waited to board a flight, and they stared at me.

A mother passed me, and her young daughter followed her several steps behind. As the young girl looked at me, her eyes opened wide and then she sprinted to catch up with her mother.

I saw my reflection in a window, and my face looked like that of a Zombie.

Sunday

It was morning in Barcelona, and a tired-looking customs officer took my passport, glanced at my photo and then at me. And then he jerked back in his seat. "What happened to you? He asked.
"An accident."

"Motorcycle?"

"No, a baseball bat."

He froze for a second, his eyebrows raised. "It is a strange sport, your baseball. You should play football."

"I agree," I said, knowing what he meant. Americans are in the minority. Around ninety-five percent of the world calls it football rather than soccer.

He handed over my passport and said, "Be careful."

I thanked him and then headed to the baggage claim area where I retrieved my backpack. After walking into the public zone, I found an information desk and asked how I could get to a town called Cadaques.

The young man behind the desk said, "Cadaques is on the Costa Brava north of Barcelona. The best option is to take a train." He pointed the way to the train station.

At a currency exchange bureau, I changed a thousand Dollars into Euros and then took the airport shuttle train to the Barcelona-Sants central train station. From there I caught a high-speed train in the direction of France. Forty-five minutes later, at the town of Figueres, I got off and hired a taxi.

The taxi went east about ten miles on a busy road. It seemed there were hundreds of cars going in the opposite direction caught in a traffic jam.

"Why are there so many cars?" I asked the driver.

"*Vacaciones de Agosto*. People go home."

"Do you mean August vacation?"

"Yes. July and August, many tourists here. *Francés, belga, alemán* and other *países*. Tomorrow it starts the first week of September and most are finish."

"Gone?"

"Yes, most are gone."

I hadn't thought of the crowds of people and began to have doubts about coming here. The last thing I needed was hordes of tourists.

At a coastal town called Rosas, the taxi turned north on an inland road, winding its way through brown hills covered with sagebrush and clusters of pine and oak trees. To the east, there was an occasional glimpse of the sea, and far away to the west were taller mountains.

After living in New York City, this felt like the middle of nowhere. Tiredness hit me. What crazy thing I had done by coming here? All this because the word *constraints* pulsated like a pack of wolves running in the back of my head.

We turned right on a road that wound down toward the sea, and after a descent of three or four miles, we came to the small town of Cadaques.

When I saw the town-sign, a strange feeling came over me, a sudden explosion of relief that I had finally arrived at my destination, yet also of anxiety. It is unsettling to go to an unknown place when your purpose in being there is vague and undefined.

The taxi pulled into a parking area, and the driver said, "Some people like to walk to hotel, to see town, or I can drive."

"How far is the hotel?" I asked.

"Maybe eight or nine hundred meters."

"I'll walk," I said, wanting to stretch my legs.

"Many streets for walking in old part of town," he said. "Go to road by seaside and turn right."

I paid the driver, thanked him, put the backpack over one shoulder and hung the computer bag over the other, and then walked to the center of the village. The weight of the bags amplified the hurt in my ribs, and

I regretted not taking the taxi to the hotel. My football player instincts took over. Play through the pain.

It was mid-afternoon, and the outside restaurants had people still finishing their lunches. They stared at me as I walked by and that reminded me of the condition of my face.

Even without those injuries, no one would select me to be a male model, with my thick body, a large head, and a slightly dented nose. Not fat. Just big. If anything, in a movie they would cast me as the meaty bodyguard of the gangster boss.

Because of my looks, I was surprised when Linette took an interest in me and when we first started going out, I questioned why she was attracted to me.

When I thought about the brutal beating in the park, it was my thick head and hefty muscular body that probably saved my life.

In the middle of Cadaques, I found a clothing shop where they sold straw hats, so I bought one while speaking miserably bad Spanish with the seller.

After coming to the road running next to the sea, I turned right. It felt good to walk. The afternoon heat combined with my pain caused me to sweat, and my shirt became damp. I stopped several times to rest. Eventually, I came to the hotel. It was next to the sea, with a hill behind it. A sign on the building said, *Hotel Casa de Los Poetas.*

I removed the backpack and computer bag from my shoulders and carried them inside where there was a small reception area. It had a dark brown tile floor matching the color of the old wood beams on the ceiling. An older woman appeared and froze when she saw me, and then she said, "*Hola.*"

"Hello," I said. "Is this where Dr. Eden gives her workshop?"

"*Si.*"

"My name is Mack McQuaid, and I signed up for it."

She pulled out a sheet of paper and looked down a small list of names, then nodded her head. She said, "Tomorrow starts the workshop." Then, from the rack behind her she took a key and handed it to me. "Room seven. Go up the stairs. Breakfast *de ocho a nueve horas. Poetas* workshop at *nueve quince*, in room there." She pointed down a hallway.

To clarify my understanding, I added, "Breakfast between eight and nine, and the workshop at nine-fifteen."

"*Si.*"

I thanked her, turned and headed for the stairs. I looked back, and the woman stood still, staring at me.

Down the hallway, I found room seven, unlocked the door and went inside. It was large with a double bed, a bathroom to one side, old-fashioned, but clean. There were two sturdy wooden chairs with red cushions on the seats, a small couch, and a coffee table, and against one wall was a bookshelf with a few poetry books in Spanish, French, and English.

One of the books was by Dr. Rachel Eden, the one mentioned in the newspaper article titled, '*The Mystery of Wisdom, Seeing through the eyes of a poet.* It was small.

Taking it down off the shelf, I quickly scanned the introduction. Dr. Eden had written that wisdom is a mystery, and she questioned why some people had more of it than others?

She classified her main points as 'Footprints', which was strange. The reasoning was that footprints determine direction. When the footprints in her book were consistently applied, they led to a life of wisdom. More than that, they provide direction for one's future. In other words, footprints determine upcoming footsteps. It was an odd concept, but it made sense. It was like a tracker in a forest who used footprints to know where someone was going.

I certainly needed wisdom for the future, because I'd been lost in a confusing forest for many months. I put her book back on the shelf thinking to get back to it when my mind was less hazy.

A few reproductions of paintings were in frames on the walls. The room had a glass door opening to a small balcony. It faced the Mediterranean Sea, with Cadaques off to the left. An old church was on the highest hill in the center of the village and stood out as the prominent feature.

I put my backpack and computer bag on the table and then went into the bathroom. When seeing myself in the mirror, horror filled me. My face was hardly recognizable, particularly the left side with the swollen eye and the band-aid covering the stitches. That side of my face was swollen, with several colors of purple, black and red. My right eye was black and blue.

I undressed, took some painkillers, reset the time on my phone to Spanish time, set the alarm, and went to bed.

My head throbbed, and it felt bizarre to be outside the comfort zone of my apartment. There can be excitement and anticipation when traveling to a new place, but once there, you feel lost. That's what I was feeling.

What looney reasoning had driven me to go halfway around the world? Doing this was insane, except that the *constraints* word kept coming back and it linked to my desolation. I was desperate to find a way out.

Footprint 2: See colors.

It is blue-butterfly day here in spring,
And with these sky-flakes down in flurry on flurry
There is more unmixed color on the wing
Than flowers will show for days unless they hurry.
Robert Frost

Monday

Ⅰn the morning, the alarm on my phone went off, and it took me a moment to remember where I was. I had slept fourteen hours. Groggy and disoriented, I showered but still couldn't shave. My face was less swollen, but the discoloration was worse than the day before.

The bandage over my stitches had become wet from the shower, and when trying to wipe away caked blood, the bandage came loose. The doctor told me to keep it on for three or four days. Unable to stick it properly back on, I removed it. There was a bloody red line running along my hairline held together by the stitches. I didn't have another bandage, so I left the cut exposed.

Hunger hit me, for I had not eaten anything since breakfast on Saturday.

I dressed in jeans and a clean t-shirt, put on my tennis shoes and went downstairs. It was a self-service breakfast, and I had a yogurt, bread with slices of cheese and three cups of black coffee. The coffee was rough for lack of a better term, but I liked it. Other diners chose tables at the opposite side of the room from me.

When finished eating, I went back to my room, and my instinct was to get my laptop and check the markets, but I left it in the computer bag. The stock markets had been my reference point for over ten years. I decided not to look at the laptop until the afternoon when the U.S. markets opened later in the day. I needed to check my account, for I had a lot of money teetering on numerous stocks. There is a fundamental rule. Don't take your eyes off the stock market when you have open positions. With an unexpected crash, you can lose everything.

At ten after nine I went downstairs and found the conference room. On one side, a window stretched across the wall facing the sea. In the front of the room was a large whiteboard, and next to it was a small table with some papers stacked on it. Four people were already in the room. Three women and a man sat behind long tables configured in a horseshoe shape. Someone had laid out five notebooks around the table, each with a pen and a pencil.

I said, "Good morning," and took a seat at the back of the room where there was a notebook.

One of the women on my left replied with, "Good morning," but the others stared at me, as though I resembled a war casualty.

The man had a smirky smile.

Soon, a tall woman walked in and took a quick look around the room, although her eyes lingered on me a bit longer than the others. I assumed this was Dr. Rachel Eden.

She wore a light pearl colored blouse and purple pants. Wrapped around her neck was a scarf, and on her feet were espadrille sandals with delicate blue leather straps. Her curly hair was turning gray. She was slim, and appeared confident, and the striking thing about her was her piercing blue eyes. Only because of the gray hair, I guessed she was around forty-five to fifty years old, although, I'm not any good at guessing ages. There was something charismatic about her, and I found her to be attractive.

With a confident voice and British accent, she said, "Please call me Rachel. I'm sure you have all read the description of this workshop on our website, so let's not waste time, other than to remind you that the workshop lasts five and a half days. You have seen that our purpose here is not to study poets or write poetry. At the same time, poetic techniques will be used to see the world in a new way. You might say that the objective is to think like a poet, but we will attempt to go beyond that."

Because of the condition I was in, I had not read the details on her website but was primarily going on the newspaper article. It was the word *constraints* that had spoken to me, and I hadn't gotten much farther than that.

She looked around the room and said, "I'd like to start by making an oversimplification, thereby establishing our direction. To generalize, let's imagine there are two groups of people. First, there are those who live by the reference points handed to them. These might come from their upbringing, their culture, and experience. It forms their belief systems and their identity. This group lives by a worldview without thinking much about it. Perhaps a better term for worldview is *lifeview*, although both terms deal with the way we perceive reality. Again, I am using this for illustrative and differentiation purposes."

I had difficulty following her.

She paused, as though not wanting to overwhelm us with information, and then continued. "In our workshop, we will explore the perspective of the second group of people. They are not easy to classify. For now, and again, for the sake of simplicity, we can call them those who truly discern. Our goal this week is to learn to be a part of the second group. In no way is this to disparage the first group or cast judgment, but it is just an observation. To break the ice, we will start with a very modest exercise, which is to observe the colors around you. Then I'd ask you to write similes and metaphors on what you have seen."

This was far outside my normal and didn't make any sense. Observing colors. What kind of a goofy activity was this?

Rachel continued. "Similes and metaphors are literary techniques used in creative writing. They make descriptions more emphatic or vivid, but they can also bring new insight. Who is familiar with them?"

Four hands went up into the air, except mine.

She looked at me and said, "It's okay if you don't know this. We all carry a different experience. To remind everyone, a simile is a comparison of one thing with another thing of a different kind. Examples would be, American as apple pie, or as big as an elephant, or to use a verse from the Book of Proverbs, a word fitly spoken is like apples of gold in pictures of silver. Each of these contains unrelated comparisons that bring out a unique perception and enhances our understanding."

She paused and looked at me, as though considering if I understood her. I didn't have a clue what she was talking about, and her explanation only made my headache worse.

She continued, "A metaphor is a bit different, but often serves the same purpose. It is a noun, where a word or phrase is applied to an object or action, although, it is not literally similar, such as the snow is a white blanket or time is money, or to use Proverbs again, the teaching of the wise is a fountain of life. In this last one, the teaching of the wise is not just any fountain, but one that gives abundance."

She explained this way too fast for me with all the noun and object business, and all those big literary words and concepts, so, I said, "I'm sorry, but I still don't get it."

Her piercing eyes gazed at me for a few seconds, and she said, "Don't worry if you don't have an academic conception of this, because that's not important for our workshop."

Looking around the room, she said, "The purpose here is not to write a perfect metaphor. It is to become observant and sensitive to the world. Please take a walk for ten minutes out on the hillside. It's a lovely day, so I believe you will find it to be an enjoyable experience. Find a comfortable place, alone, and reflect only on the colors you see around you. The question is, how many different colors do you see?"

That was a bizarre question, and I felt like taking another painkiller. What did seeing different colors have to do with dealing with constraints?

She said, "In one of his poems, Robert Frost said there were more colors to be noticed in the wings of a butterfly than in the spring flowers. That is an amazing eye. Therefore, I'm asking you to try and do the same. Spend adequate time to distinguish every unique color. **See colors**. Colors are everywhere, but like so many other details, we don't notice them. And, in so doing, we have tuned out our ability to discern."

During the past months, the primary color surrounding my life was gray, other than the red and green on my computer monitor, red when a stock position was making a loss, and green when it was profitable.

"Once you've done that, reflect on a few of the colors you have identified, and then write some similes and metaphors like the examples I gave you. Any allegory will do. Use the notebooks in front of you to jot down your thoughts. We will meet back here at eleven fifteen."

She quickly walked out of the room.

I looked at the other participants. They were smiling.

The guy exclaimed, "This is so cool."

The three women looked at him and grinned.

Something had ignited their passion, but I certainly didn't know what it was.

They scampered away, and I looked around the empty room, confused by what we were assigned to do. Eventually, I picked up the notebook, pen, and pencil.

Once outside the *Casa de Los Poetas,* I considered heading for town to get a coffee. Then, I turned and walked on a road to the west, winding up a hill. The other participants were far ahead of me.

Five minutes later, out of breath and sweating, I found a lone pine tree and sat down in the shade. My body was stiff and sore from the beating in the park and the long airplane ride. It was still the middle of the night in New York City, and I was disoriented.

I opened the notebook and held the pen, and then looked at the scenery, brown hills, a picturesque village off to the left, with old houses and tile roofs, and a shining sea reflecting the sun. The morning was already hot, and I wondered what it would feel like in the afternoon.

I tried to think of a simile but still didn't know the difference between a simile and a metaphor. Dr. Rachel Eden said anything would do. Then, the entire exercise seemed silly. What difference would it make in real life if you could think in metaphors and similes?

In reflecting on this weird workshop, I considered that the *constraints* word might not be that important anymore. The poet Doctor Rachel walked into the room and spoke for maybe five minutes, and then she sent us out to ponder our navels for a couple of hours. This course cost money. Was it nothing more than a scam?

* * *

It was mindboggling to think that a large corporation would allow employees to splurge on expensive flights to Spain, and then sit around on a dry, dusty hill doing nothing, with the pretense of releasing them from the constraints through which they saw the world. Honestly, I needed to be freed from the prison of my apartment, but was it necessary to sit under a pine tree?

In the newspaper article, those marketing guys claimed they had become more creative and sensitive. They had learned to imagine. That sounded ridiculous. Marketing people typically didn't lack creativity or imagination, so what more could this workshop give them?

This workshop was a bad idea, so I considered going somewhere else, but it had taken considerable effort to get here, and I didn't have the energy to go anywhere else. Hopping on a train to see Europe was out of the question. I probably wouldn't enjoy it. My head hurt, and I required quietness over the next few days. Having already paid for the workshop, why not stay and get some rest?

The objective of the assignment still wasn't clear. Rachel said, to look at colors and then write about them, such as a white blanket is like snow or something like that.

For a moment, I looked for colors around me, in the sky and the sea and the old buildings of Cadaques. But quickly, my mind wandered from colors to random thoughts of trading stocks, and Linette, and my limited lifestyle over the past months. Why was I so stuck when I had the financial resources to do just about anything?

I shifted my weight and laid back on the pine needles. That gave relief to my sore ribs. The pain caused me to think of the random beating, and that question came to me. One of the two guys said, "Goodbye, Mack." How did he know my name? Because of that, it was evident that the attack was not random. Therefore, maybe it was good to stay away from New York City, at least until my body healed.

An hour and a half later it was time to go back to the conference room, and I hadn't put a single word in the notebook. Then, I looked down at a brown pine needle in front of me and rapidly wrote my first simile. Or, was it a metaphor?

After quickly making up a couple more I went back to the conference room and took my place. The other participants arrived shortly after me, and then Rachel came into the room.

Once everyone was seated, Rachel stood at the front, and said, "Would you be willing to share your metaphors? We will go around the room, and please tell us your name, and a little about yourself. Then you can share your findings, but only if you want to."

Earlier in the morning, I hadn't noticed much about the other participants, as I had been self-absorbed.

Rachel nodded to a young woman on her right.

The young woman said, "My name is Patricia Younger, and a year ago I completed a Master's Degree in Creative Writing. Since then, I've been suffering from writer's block. Hopefully, the workshop might help." She had expressive brown eyes and dark brunette hair.

Heads nodded around the room.

"Here are three I came up with," she said.

Blue like a distant dream.
Red like desperately broken tiles.
Green as a weed in rocks with worried hope.

Rachel gave a small smile, and the rest of the participants grinned.

The next woman named Diana had taught English at a high school and was taking a break from teaching. She seemed younger than me, perhaps in her late twenties or early thirties. She had blond hair and blue eyes, and when she smiled, she lit up the room.

One of Diana's similes was,

Yellow as a pungent sunbeam.

Again, everyone grinned.

I was next, and I said, "I'm Mack McQuaid and am in between jobs." They didn't need to know that I had walked out of managing a mutual fund and currently was a hermit day-trader. I read out my three.

Brown like a brown pine needle.
Blue sea like deep blue water.
Blue sky like with clouds.

The room went into a still silence, and the guy on my right broke out in laughter, and the other participants smiled. My head throbbed from the concussion, and their hilarity only augmented the pain. Except for required courses in high school, I avoided English classes, preferring Economics and Business. Similes and metaphors were foreign.

"Very interesting," Rachel said. "Let's move on."

The guy spoke out. "Those aren't similes or anything. They unquestionably don't make a description more emphatic or vivid."

Rachel took a deep breath, waited a few seconds, and then said, "May I remind everyone that we are not here to master literary techniques. What's important is how you see."

The guy looked at her with quizzical eyes, as though he missed something. He then introduced himself. His name was Barry, and he taught at a Junior College in California.

I guessed Barry was a bit younger than me. He was tall, lean, and muscular. His dark hair was combed back on his head which accentuated his masculine face. I supposed his mannish looks, combined with his blue eyes would make him attractive to women.

Barry claimed he could write similes and metaphors all day long. His were,

Blue like the sea of a dream.
Brown in hue as hazel nuts.
Red as with wine out of season.

The women participants focused on every word, although, Rachel frowned, and Diana looked perplexed.

Then Barry said, "I have more," and without the go-ahead from Rachel, he said,

The purple wound of painful hopelessness.
The remorseless black eyes of depravity.
The red line above a missing void.

He looked at me and grinned. Patricia, Diana and the third woman on my right glanced at me and then looked away with uncomfortable smiles. Rachel looked at Barry with questioning eyes. Then, I understood he was speaking about the condition of my face.

The last person, the young woman on my right, also had a Master's Degree in English Literature. Her name was Jade, and she had graduated three years previously from an East Coast ivy league college. She was slender, and maybe in her mid-twenties. There was something fragile about her, yet she seemed energetic like she had a strong will.

Jade shared two of her similes.

Blue as pendulous paradise.
Dust red like protective sheaths.

That ended the first morning, and we broke for lunch. As I left the room, I wondered what practical value this session had. It could never apply to stock trading. What good did it do to notice colors? Who cares if something is yellow, red, or blue, or any other shade in the color wheel?

* * *

We had lunch at a large round table on the terrace next to the dining room. A giant umbrella provided shade.

I wore sunglasses and my straw hat, as the summer sun only made my headache worse.

The meal was paella, a traditional Spanish dish made with rice and various kinds of meat, fish and shrimp cooked on a large, round shallow pan.

They served chilled rosé wine with the meal, but I took *agua con gaz*, carbonated water.

Barry sat across from me, and he became the center of the conversation. I had difficulty in chewing my food because of pain in my jaw, so concentrated on eating rather than talking.

The conversation quickly shifted into literary things.

Barry asked, "Do you put the adverb before or after the verb?"

"What do you mean?" Diana asked.

"For instance, do you say ran quickly or quickly ran?"

"It depends on the meaning," Patricia stated.

"I'm not sure," Jade remarked, "Especially when you have the case of a split infinitive."

"No," Barry said, "I think Patricia is correct. You need to ask questions about the sense and ambiguity of the sentence, to determine if the adverb comes before or after."

The conversation went on like this through the entire meal. At times they got into friendly debates with everyone talking at the same time. They argued about allegories, hyperboles, parables and puns, and whether these should even be considered metaphors. Each person had a different classification method.

I was lost.

Then, they got even more excited when talking about writers and poets who were recently featured in literary journals. My fellow students were like fans idolizing rock stars. I didn't know any of the names they mentioned, and it seemed they spoke a foreign language.

They appeared to be in a bubble of literary pomposity that had little to do with the real world. Eventually, I tuned them out.

Toward the end of the meal, Barry spoke up. "Hey Mack, could I ask you a question?"

I raised my head and asked, "What's that?"

"It is Mack, right?"

"Yes."

"Who calls their kid that? But, that's not my question."

"What's your question?" Mack McQuaid is on my birth certificate with no middle name and no father mentioned, but he didn't need to know that.

"What happened?" Barry asked.

"What happened, where?"

"There." He pointed at the left side of my face.

"Oh that," I said. "Baseball bat."

"What?" Barry exclaimed.

Jade interjected, "That's terrible. Were you in a baseball game?"

"No, it was something different, but no big deal."

"No big deal," Jade countered. "Your face is like hamburger."

"Is that a simile or a metaphor?" I tried to smile.

She laughed. "Anything with the word 'like' is a simile. But really, you must be in pain."

"It hurts," I stated. "It hurts like . . . ah, like I don't know what. This metaphor business is new to me."

Diana asked, "Are you taking medicine?

"Painkillers and anti-inflammatory pills."

"Careful," Barry said. "You can become addicted. Don't become a crack-head, but I guess you already are, after looking at that those stitches." He laughed.

"That's not funny," Patricia said.

I raised my hand. "It's alright. I suffered a concussion, so maybe it is funny."

"Oh, my goodness," Diana remarked. "You should be resting."

"I'm okay." I couldn't tell them that in the grand scope of things, the last months had been worse than a concussion.

"Why are you taking this workshop?" Diana asked.

"I don't know. I saw something in the newspaper and thought it might be interesting." I certainly couldn't tell them I was here because of constraints and my miserable lifestyle, which was all my own doing. I wasn't addicted to drugs. I was addicted to living in a box. "Why are you here?" I asked Diana.

"For a number of years I've been teaching high school students, who for the most part could care less about English or any other subject. It gets to you because sometimes the results seem small for all the effort put into it. Is that what I want to do with the rest of my life? I thought this workshop might give a new perspective."

"Makes sense," I said. I turned to Patricia. "And you, what's your motivation?"

"Writer's block. I don't have any new ideas." As she said it, her golden brown eyes drifted down to the table, as lights dimming.

Patricia and Diana were like me, needing a new viewpoint. "How about you, Jade?"

She laughed. "My parents paid for a month of travel in Europe, on the condition that I do something constructive during my time here. The poetry workshop met their conditions. I was happy with a job I had, but they didn't like it and put unbelievable pressure on me, and I caved in. The result was a free trip to Europe for attending an easy workshop in the Spanish sun. But, I regret the whole thing."

It seemed that Jade's goal was not to discover a new viewpoint, so she was in a different category than Diana, Patricia and me. I turned to Barry. "How about you? Was your name Larry?"

Barry glared at me. "It's Barry. I'm here for the experience. This course is for creative people with literary interests. If I may speak honestly, Mack, you may consider that this workshop is outside your field. Did you say you were in-between?"

"That's correct," I answered.

"In-between what?"

"I'm looking for my next challenge." It felt flat when I said it.

"But, what's your field of study or job experience?"

"I did some business."

"Capitalism?" Barry asked.

"You might call it that."

"Oh, your poor lost soul." He looked at me as though I was the devil.

"I moved on from that," I said.

"Moved on?"

"More like walked out."

"Whatever. Even so, you might consider that this workshop is not right for you."

"Thanks for your input, but I'll hang around for a while."

"Good luck," he said. He stood up and said to the women. "I think they are serving coffee on the lower terrace. Shall we go?"

Everyone left, and I sat alone realizing that was the most extended conversation I had with anyone over the past six months. I also sensed that Barry was like some egotistical people in the financial world. I guess you find them in every walk of life.

* * *

We had an hour before going back to the conference room, so I went up to my room and laid down on my bed. My head throbbed. It was bizarre that such a simple exercise of looking at colors had worn me out. Or, was it the lunch and having to converse with people? Or, was it Barry? I wondered if I could put up with him for the entire week.

I didn't know much about the literary world and the people in it. In university, I had the impression that English majors were goofy-headed, lazy, and full of personal issues. Their courses consisted of reading old novels. They were incapable of finding real jobs.

When I read the newspaper article and then booked this course, I assumed business teams would be here. Now I was disappointed to find a group of screwy English Lit people who got excited about sitting on a dry, dusty hill to write meaningless slogans about colors. What was their motivation?

With my head resting on the pillow, I tried to sleep, but something was off, either from jet-lag or the physical condition of my body. I looked at the walls and ceiling of my room. The building was old, and it seemed that endless buckets of white paint were layered on the walls over the years, so the texture was like silky cream. Close to one of the paintings on the wall, someone had smashed a mosquito. It was outstretched as though making angel images in the snow.

When I shifted my weight on the bed, it creaked like a growling animal.

I wondered what Dr. Rachel would ask us to do in the next session. Would it be another one of those artsy-fartsy assignments?

Footprint 3: Sense creation.

They see the Form of Air; but mortals breathing it
Drink the whole summer down into the breast.
The lavish pinks, the field new-mown, the ravishing
Sea-smells, the wood-fire smoke that whispers Rest.
        C.S. Lewis

I was born on the prairie and the milk of its wheat, the red of its
clover, the eyes of its women, gave me a song and a slogan.
*   Here the water went down, the icebergs slid with gravel, the gaps*
and the valleys hissed, and the black loam came, and the yellow sandy
loam.
        Carl Sandburg

After the lunch break, we assembled back into the conference room. Rachel walked in, waited a moment until she had everyone's attention, and then said, "Some of you may wonder about this morning's exercise. For an artist, choosing the right color is essential, but picking colors is not our purpose. I gave this exercise for a completely different reason. It is to take notice of the world around you. So often we ignore the details. By learning to observe, we gain insight. We expand that insight by equating an object or concept to something similar or different. This develops our ability to think and perceive. When we do this, we expand our ability to discern, which is an element of wisdom."

She paused, as though allowing time for that thought to sink in. Previously, I had asked myself what practical purpose this exercise had. Now, I understood where she might be going. My mindset over the past months had been narrowing rather than expanding.

Rachel said, "This afternoon will be a repeat of this morning where we used the sense of sight. Now you will use your remaining senses to perceive your environment. Find a different place and see what you discover. **Sense creation.** Dig below the normal and search for something new. What's most important is to try and experience your senses in a new way. We often ignore our senses. Now is the moment to employ them in their fullness."

The only thing I felt about creation was the ache in my muscles, tendons, and bones.

She took a moment to look at each participant, then said, "Develop that into similes and metaphors, and we will meet back here in two hours."

Heads nodded and faces grinned. Rachel turned to leave the room, and the other participants started to get up.

I said, "I don't understand."

Rachel stopped, and the others stood behind the tables and looked at me.

"What do you mean, to perceive the environment?" I asked.

With a slight smile, she said, "It's just a way of asking you to sense what is going on around you. For instance, if you say, 'fresh sea breezes', it is a metaphor that reflects the senses, in this case, freshness to your skin. If you say, 'the wind roared like a lion', it is a simile that expresses pressure from the wind. How often do you feel nature around you, and I mean to experience its splendid magnificence? By becoming aware of your senses, you will better discern the world. Does that answer your question?"

"I think so," I answered, knowing I didn't sense much. How can you feel anything when the significant person in your life has reduced you to rubble?

Rachel nodded and then left the room.

The day was hot, so I went back to the same tree as in the morning. I wore my straw hat and had changed from jeans to shorts. I removed the band-aids off my knees. Besides gooey blood, there was yellow, runny, pussy gook oozing from the scrapes. The air and sun would help dry them out.

After so many months of hunkering down in my apartment, my skin was pasty white, and I was concerned about getting a sunburn.

Honestly, I was getting fed up with this touchy-feely business, and we were barely half-way through the first day.

My head hurt, and it felt like a clanging church bell. A concussion is nothing to take lightly. It is a brain injury, and besides a headache, other symptoms include drowsiness and lack of attention. I was suffering from all of those. Jetlag was also kicking in big time.

The sun was bright, and sweat covered my shirt. A light breeze blew in from the sea, but one could not call it refreshing. Moped noises came from the village of Cadaques. A passenger jet was high in the sky, leaving a vapor trail behind it, but it made no sound. Other than that, I didn't notice anything in the so-called environment, let alone feel anything.

Again, I thought about Rachel. She had spent about three minutes explaining what to do. When I calculated what we paid for the time she gave us, her fees were higher than any big-time management consultant. She had a good thing going here, but I couldn't say that my customer satisfaction rating was high.

I tried to think of similes and metaphors. Nothing came, so I laid on my back on the pine needles, pulled my hat low over my head and went into a deep sleep.

Sometime later I woke up, looked at the time on my phone and saw that I had slept for two hours. We were supposed to be back in the room.

I tried to run back to the hotel but the pain in my body didn't allow that, so I slowed down and took my time. Even so, my t-shirt became sweaty under my armpits and down my back.

When I entered the room, everyone stared at me. I said, "Sorry for being late."

Barry rolled his eyes. Patricia was reading out her last simile,

Whispers of wind.

Diana gave three,

The sun is a torch to the soul.
The sea is a bitter-sweet breath.
The wind carries swallows as free spirits across borders.

Diana's metaphors were about the world around us, the so-called environment. It was true, there had been swallows in the air, and I hardly noticed them. There was something pleasant in her jingle about swallows. Someone could use it in a commercial.

It was my turn, and I had not written anything down, so I made up three on the spot.

Hot day, no air, no fan.
Today is a skin burner.
Distant noises like there's no way to tell.

The room went silent, and there were muffled giggles. Barry said, "Man, for sure, you don't belong here."

The women participants turned to see how Rachel would respond. She looked at me, at Barry, and then peered at the other participants. Taking her time, she said, "Please remember that the purpose of this workshop is not about literary correctness. It is not about techniques and vocabulary. It is something different. While techniques and vocabulary are helpful, our purpose here is about perception, which then opens the door to many things. It's how we see the world, leading to the way we think, act, communicate and create. Of course, the fundamental question is whether there is one right way to see reality or many ways? But, that is philosophical and religious, and now is not the time to explore this. For now, our purpose is different. It is merely to become more attentive to the world. Let's move on." She looked at Barry.

He gazed around the room, stopping to stare into the eyes of each participant as if trying to achieve a dramatic effect. When he had everybody's attention, he said,

Heats like the hammered anvil.

He paused, and I wondered if he was expecting an Academy Award. After taking a deep breath, he continued,

Soft as the melody of youthful days.
Hot as a swinked gypsy.

Patricia and Jade gazed at Barry as though a god had blessed them. Diana had that same quizzical look on her face as in the morning. Worry lines appeared on Rachel's forehead, and it seemed like she held back from saying something. Then, Rachel looked at Jade and nodded.
Jade said,

The sun is a bright golden coin I can never grasp.
The ant crawled on my leg like a lost explorer.
Shade shelters like an imaginary lover.

Patricia and Diana grinned in appreciation.
Barry turned to Jade and said, "I like the bit about a lover. That's a fantasy to consider."
She shook her head and rolled her eyes.
I thought she had done well for someone who was only in the workshop for a comfortable week in the Spanish sun.
Rachel said, "Today we opened a door. The purpose is to intensify your awareness of the external world through all your senses. It is to become more cognizant of colors, sounds, and touch. It is to experience the wind and sun. We use senses to perceive the dynamics around us. We expand that perception by equating our senses to something that may

seem unrelated, like shade associated with a lover. I found Jade's metaphor to be beautiful."

Jade lowered her eyes and slightly blushed.

Rachel said, "Patricia and Diana, your whispers of wind and the sea as a bitter-sweet breath are lovely illustrations. And, Mack, the term skin burner is raw and real. I was surprised that none of you spoke about the sense of smell. And, no one mentioned the sense of taste. By becoming more sensitive to all these God-given gifts, sight, touch, hearing, smell, and taste, we can better perceive what is real. By combining these senses with unrelated concepts, it expands our imagination and enhances our understanding. That's the end of today's session, but your journey has just begun. As you enjoy your meal this evening, take time to appreciate the myriad of textures and colors and tastes. Equate them with something that augments your experience. Your life will be richer for it. Tomorrow we will explore the inner world."

Rachel turned and walked out of the room. It was then that I noticed her posture. It was straight and strong and confident, with the grace of a dancer.

Everyone else left the room, and I put my elbows on the table and rested my head in my hands. The day was exhausting. I had not had this much contact with people in months. This workshop was far outside my routines and much more tiring than concentrating on stock markets for sixteen hours a day. That was a reminder that I needed to check my trading account.

I went back to my room, got my laptop and connected to the hotel's Wi-Fi. After logging into my trading account, I saw it was down ten thousand dollars. No big deal, but I don't like to lose in this game. The markets had dropped. When that happens, there are always opportunities. My instinct was to go through my analysis algorithms.

In looking at the stock charts, they suggested the drop was temporary, but charts can be false friends. Anything can tip the markets, and I mean anything. A politician says something, a storm hits an oil refinery, or the orange crop in Florida freezes, and the markets go topsy-turvy. To successfully trade the markets, one must keep a constant eye on a myriad of interconnected variables.

I opened a financial news website and suddenly stopped. Is this what I wanted? I knew the answer. This addiction was destroying me. Then, I considered that someone could get addicted to just about anything, even to poetry.

Just before closing the financial news website, I caught a headline, Hedge Fund Goes Bust. Manager Jailed. I was tempted to open the article and read more but clicked off. There was no way to combine a stock market obsession with a poetry workshop. Most importantly, I needed my wounds to heal. So, I decided not to trade stocks for the rest of the week.

I took one last quick look at my portfolio before turning off the laptop. The total value in my account was in the millions but did it matter?

I put the laptop back in my computer bag, laid down on the bed and noticed a new pain. I was sunburned. Then I fell asleep and entered into confused dreams of stock markets and suffering, and a bed that growled, and a metaphor that the sun is like a skin burner. Sensual, seductive Linette weaved in and out, and that left me in torment.

* * *

Tuesday

After another fourteen-hours of restless sleep, a cold shower in the morning cleared the fuzziness from my brain. I still couldn't shave, but the swelling on my face had gone down, and the purple was turning to yellow. I touched my face, and it was less sore, but my ribs still hurt.

I went to the dining room, got black coffee and a croissant and found a table. As I drank my coffee, Patricia came in. She put food on a tray, looked around the room and then hesitated. I waved and pointed to the place opposite me. She came over and sat down.

"Good morning," I said.

"Good morning." Her voice was weak.

"How was your sleep? I always find it takes a while to adjust to a new bed," I stated.

She smiled. "That describes the last five weeks."

"What do you mean?" I asked.

"I went from youth hostel to youth hostel. It wears you out."

Her eyes seemed focused on a faraway land, and I realized that I had not taken much notice of her before, the color of her hair, her eyes, or her expressions.

The morning light softly reflected off her face and dark hair. She was striking. I asked, "Where have you been?"

"What do you mean?"

"Where were you during the past five weeks?"

"I had a train pass and went all over the place, visiting as many art museums as I could across the continent. To save money, I slept quite a few nights on trains."

"Were you on your own?"

"Yes. That was a mistake." She looked at my chest and arms and then smiled. "I could have used someone like you."

"What do you mean?"

"Everywhere, guys trying to . . . ah, meet me. You could have helped."

I laughed. "You mean, my looks would have scared them off?"

She smiled. "That, and of course your size."

"I was a linebacker on my university football team, six-four, two hundred and thirty pounds, and quick."

"Did you consider going professional?"

"I did, but with a weak knee, it seemed less hazardous to go to graduate school. Now, look at me." I pointed at my face.

She raised her eyebrows. "You said you're between jobs?"

"That's correct."

"So somehow, you end up here."

"I know. A crazy poetry workshop is a strange place to be." I didn't want to go into the *constraints* word, and all that it meant. "How are you finding this experience so far?"

She said, "It's only just begun. I'm hoping it will help. People in the literary world are talking about Rachel and her new book is quite provocative."

"You mean, *The Mystery of Wisdom*?"

"Yes, but it's the subtitle that intrigues me, *The Lost Art of Perceiving Like a Poet.*"

I nodded. "It's not something that most people think about."

"Exactly, although at this point in my life I need a little wisdom because I feel stuck. It's frustrating. I completed a graduate school degree in creative writing, yet nothing creative comes out of my head. I finished a novel but am unable to advance it from there. Some people call it writer's block. I call it, life-block. It's like being shoehorned into a mummy casket. Maybe I should forget the whole thing and chart a different course. So, I need to figure out what to do next."

Her eyes dipped when she said this. I hesitated and then asked, "Is there something more than the novel?"

She shook her head back and forth and whispered, "Guys."

"Oh," was all I could say. I am one.

She stared at the table as though I wasn't there, and said, "How can I put it? It's painful to be objectified, lied to, used and dumped."

"I understand," I replied, knowing I should have said, join the club.

It made me uncomfortable, Patricia sharing herself like that. I was good at analyzing company balance sheets, but not particularly good with people. The conversation at lunch the previous day was the most extended discussion I had had in six months. This one with Patricia was not about the weather. It was about her feelings and something deep inside, and that made me nervous.

"Are you going to be okay?" I asked.

She took a deep breath, looked at me, and I sensed she was on the edge of tears. "I hope so," she said, "Being here provides a safe break."

"If there's anything I can do for you, please let me know." That felt strange coming out of my mouth, for I had not done anything good for anyone in a long time.

"Thank you," she replied. "You are a kind person."

I smiled, again not knowing how to respond.

She composed herself, and said, "By the way, I recently took a class in sketching, hoping it would help me with writer's block. I draw people and hope you don't mind that I sketched you."

"Me?"

"I'm embarrassed to show it."

I smiled. "It's probably not pretty."

She grinned. "You make a unique model." She reached into her notebook and handed me her drawing.

I laughed. "It's prettier than I thought, but a bit too serious,"

"You are serious," she said.

"I'm missing an ear."

She looked at the drawing, and said, "Oops." Then she looked at me. "No, it's okay. Your hair was covering your ear."

"The stitches give me a macho look, although the actual bruise under my left eye is far bigger and more horrid than that."

"I know. I need to practice drawing bruises."

"It looks like one of those police crime sketches. Maybe you have a future?"

"That's the last thing I'd want to do." She grinned.

I said, "Six feet four, and two hundred and thirty pounds of pure ugliness."

"Next time I'll improve on it."

"You better," I joked.

"Please forgive me for doing this without your permission."

"It's okay. I like it." It had been a long time since anyone did anything for me and it touched me more than she knew.

She handed me the sketch, and we got up from the table just as Jade and Barry came into the dining room. They went straight to the coffee machine. From their red eyes, it looked like they had a sleepless night.

Footprint 4: Tune in to feelings.

cautiously, I allowed
myself to feel good
at times.
I found moments of
peace in cheap
rooms
just staring at the
knobs of some
dresser
or listening to the
rain in the
dark.
the less i needed
the better i
felt.
Charles Bukowski

All participants were in the conference room at nine-fifteen, and Rachel walked in. After greeting us and discussing the previous day's exercises, she said, "Yesterday was a beginning, a footprint."

The term, footprint, had been used in Rachel's book on wisdom, so I understood what she meant by it, but it still seemed weird.

She said, "Today we continue our quest to see the world differently. To achieve this goal, we can learn from poets."

I'd prefer to learn from an economist than a poet.

She said, "Yesterday was external, that is, sensing the world around us. Today we turn to the internal. I'd like you to . . ."

"I want to pose a question," Barry demanded.

Rachel glanced out toward the sea, then looked at Barry. "Not now, please," she answered.

Barry gasped. "Why not?"

"Questions are for another time," Rachel stated. "As I was saying, our goal is to look inward and not outward. What are you feeling at this moment in time? Think about how you physically feel but go beyond that. Try to get in touch with yourself. Dig deep if necessary to discover your feelings at the current moment. Once identified, take those feelings and create metaphors. These can lead to insights."

Rachel walked out of the room.

The speed with which she explained this was way too fast. It left me confused. She was messing with our heads.

We all stood up, and as we left the room, Barry said, "That's ridiculous that we can't ask questions. Her teaching method is lame."

Jade nodded in polite agreement, but she quickly picked up her notepad and walked out of the room.

I was the last one to leave and noticed that Jade, Patricia, and Barry headed for the hills. Instead of going in that direction, I walked to the village of Cadaques, found a store and bought a bottle of sunscreen. Then I went to a coffee bar, sat down at an outside table in the shade and ordered a coffee. People at another table had a small basket with bread with grated tomato. So, I discretely pointed and said to the waiter, "I'd like that."

He said, "*Pan con tomate.*"

He left, and a few minutes later he came back and placed the coffee and bread with tomato on my table. It was toasted and covered with olive oil, grated tomato, and garlic. I devoured it. My appetite was coming back.

The outside table was as good a place as any to think about feelings. I applied the sunscreen to my legs, arms and face, and sipped the coffee.

Rachel asked us to think about how we were currently feeling. I felt sore. She said we should go beyond the physical, but that wasn't easy. Other than feeling beat up and jetlagged, I couldn't identify any other emotions. It was like they were nonexistent or buried in a pit.

My thought drifted to the other participants. I felt sorry for Patricia, because of what she had shared, and didn't particularly like Barry. Jade was an unknown.

How was I currently feeling? I didn't know. Feelings were not part of my daily life. When trading stocks, I went on facts and made deductions based on logic. For sure, sometimes I had a feeling about where to place an investment, but that was mostly grounded in experience. It's risky to base vital decisions only on opinions or emotions, but that isn't what Rachel was suggesting. She was merely asking us to get in touch with ourselves, which I suppose was not such a bad thing.

As far as feelings from the past, there was only one word that came up, especially from the last six months. It was the word, *numb*. I quickly wrote down three similes on my notepad. Or, were they metaphors?

From the café bar, I had a good view of the Sea. Cadaques was at the end of a bay, with small fishing boats pulled up on the sandy beaches and yachts anchored in the bay. The town wasn't crowded with people, but it wasn't deserted.

While watching people, I saw Rachel walking quickly on the road next to the sea. Next to her was another woman who carried a thin, rectangular package wrapped in brown paper. The other woman was younger than Rachel and taller, yet there was something similar about them.

The younger woman had long thick brunette hair, the sun glistening off light streaks. With a graceful movement, she raised her hand and moved strands of hair away from her face. As she did this, she glanced at me with confident eyes, holding her gaze for a moment, her face having a curious expression like an artist considering the subject of a painting. Then she turned and continued walking down the street next to Rachel. They both walked with a sense of confidence and determination.

Men and women seated at the tables watched them. Then the two women turned down a small street and disappeared. I wondered what Rachel was doing in town and thought again about the workshop. She had a good thing going here. While all the participants worked, she was strolling around town.

Then I saw Diana carrying a shopping bag, so I waved at her. She came over to my table, smiled and asked, "Playing hooky from the exercise?"

I laughed. "Not really. The instruction was to find a place to reflect on your innards. Here is as good a place as any."

"Then, I won't bother you," she said.

"No. I finished the assignment. Please join me. Would you like something to drink?"

She sat down, and I ordered a *café con leche* for her, coffee with milk, and then asked, "Did you complete your jingles?"

"Jingles?"

"Yes, your similes and whatnot."

She laughed. "It didn't take long. I've been in the English Literature game for a long time, and my feelings are easy to identify. Therefore, I quickly put the pieces together. How about you?"

"It didn't take me long either."

She hesitated and then asked, "Can you share what you discovered?"

"Oh, it's simple. I discovered nothing."

"Nothing?"

"Connecting to the touchy-feely side is difficult for me."

She leaned toward me, her blue eyes expressing the concern of a mother. "Why is that?"

"Good question. Maybe it's due to my childhood. Maybe the sports I played. Maybe my job. Maybe I was taught that men shouldn't have feelings."

"So, you suppress them," she stated.

"I guess." I didn't want her to learn the real reason, but she was probably right. The last six months had been a suppression as I had retracted into my self-imposed exile.

Her coffee came, so I thought it was an excellent opportunity to deflect the conversation. I asked, "What did you discover about yourself?"

"Oh, there's not much to discover. I know what I'm feeling. As I mentioned yesterday, I've been a school teacher. It is something I enjoy, but recently I ran out of energy. So, I decided to take a year off to evaluate my life."

"Have you made any discoveries?"

"It's only been two months since the end of the school year, but I'm struggling to know if my life should go in another direction."

"Why's that?"

She glanced at a couple walking on the road by the sea. They held hands, and her eyes lingered on them. She said. "It's difficult to share."

I smiled and responded, "It's okay. No pressure. Feel free with me."

She hesitated, took a sip of coffee, put the cup on the table, and said, "My emotions are unsettled. I met a man, Peter, who is a doctor. He lost his spouse several years ago, like me. We immediately felt a bond, but it was more than that. We enjoy being with each other, we have similar tastes and desires for life, and we share a common faith."

"How did you meet?"

"He and his two children were at their home in Florida for the summer. That's where I live. We met at my church, and I clicked with him and the two kids, a young teen and a pre-teen. After two months of being with them, he proposed marriage, and then he and his children had to return to Africa. That's where he runs a hospital, as a surgeon and a missionary. When they left, I came here."

"Then, what's the problem?" I asked.

"I'm unable to make the step. You see, three years ago I went through terrible pain, and I can't get over it. My husband went fishing on a boat with a couple of friends, they got hit by a storm, and the three of them were lost at sea, their bodies never found." The happy countenance was gone from her face.

"That's tough," I said. "I'm sorry for you."

"You see that water over there?" She pointed at the bay. 'Every time I get around the sea, whether it is the Atlantic Ocean or the Mediterranean Sea, I think of my husband. You don't know how difficult it is when your loved one disappears from one moment to the next."

I remembered her metaphor from the workshop, that, *the sea is a bitter-sweet breath.* Now it had meaning. "I cannot imagine," I said, knowing disappearances can happen in other ways.

"I'm not sure I could go through that pain again, to lose someone. And underneath it all, I carry a deep question."

"What's that?" I felt my responses were short and shallow, inadequate to meet the depth of emotion she was feeling.

"How could God allow that to happen? Combined with that, every day I blame myself for what happened to my husband, for letting him go fishing that day, knowing a storm was nearby."

"I'm not sure you should blame yourself, but as far as the God question, that's out of my league."

She made one quick laughing sound, almost a loud exhale. "Yes, that's a big one and the answer is elusive. So, in a nutshell, that's what's behind my feelings, hope for a new family, love for my doctor friend, and fear that destroys all my joy."

"Could you move to Africa?"

"Of course. In a heartbeat. As I said before, I'm ready for a change. Peter's kids are great, and I could teach English in a local school. It's all positive, but I carry this invisible weight and am unable to get rid of it."

I knew about weights, having one so heavy that I felt numb. I didn't know what to say and was probably the last person to give advice. I said, "It's alleged this poetry workshop gives a new perspective on things. Maybe it will help."

"I hope so," she said.

I do too, I said to myself.

* * *

We gathered back in the conference room, and Rachel took her place. She said, "To gain maximum benefit from this workshop, may I say something that could sound controversial? The purpose is to help avoid going in a wrong direction. Let me say it like this. Some poets are not real poets, at least in regard to our objective."

"How can that be?" Barry asked.

Rachel looked at him and nodded. "Please let me clarify because this is critical for our success. Academically, we train students to use the right techniques, so they become masters at creating pithy sayings and forming abstract literary constructions. Our goal is different."

"So, in your opinion, what's a real poet?" Barry asked.

"I believe there are several characteristics. One is that poets, real poets, have a way of expanding the way we look at the world. It's not just putting together charming or highbrow phrases. Real poets give a deeper perception. Does that make sense?" She looked around the room.

Several heads nodded.

I thought that poetry was nothing more than saying things in complicated ways.

Rachel continued, "There's another characteristic that I'll speak about later in the week, and that is, real poets have a way of bringing out the truth."

"So, you are going to turn us into real poets," Barry said with a mocking tone."

"That's up to you. As I said before, this workshop is to help you think like a poet, but also to go beyond that, even to deal with beliefs. Everyone has a way of looking, a worldview or lifeview for lack of a better terms. Belief systems are built upon that. Sometimes those worldviews can become narrow or irrelevant or can even lead to a destructive path. Therefore, it can be helpful to discover a new way of seeing."

It seemed an odd shift. Rachel jumped from poets to worldviews. This was puzzling.

Barry spoke up. "Can I ask another question? What difference does it make if we see the world in a new way?"

Rachel scanned the faces in the room, paused and said, "That's an interesting question and gets into philosophy, which is a long discussion. So, if you don't mind, I'll take no more questions. What's important now are the questions you ask yourself."

"What? This is bull," Barry stated. "We paid hard cash for this workshop, so we should be able to ask questions."

It seemed Barry was attempting to derail the class from Rachel's purpose for the session.

Rachel gave a small smile. "You can have your cash back anytime you want, minus hotel nights and meals."

Barry sat in tense silence."

Rachel continued. "Now, I was saying that sometimes it is helpful to challenge our thinking. In Clinical Psychology, a field I know, one goal is to help people see their situation in a new way, and most often this involves thinking beyond boundaries."

Everyone stared at Rachel, except for Barry whose head was down, his eyes narrowed.

Rachel continued. "Yesterday we looked externally by using our senses, and this morning we went internal by exploring our feelings. Please feel free to share what you discovered, or if you prefer not to share, that's perfectly alright. Your feelings belong to you. No one is obliged."

Patricia looked at the notebook in front of her, hesitated, and then opened it. She said, "I wrote many, but here are two."

She took a deep breath and then read her similes.

Abused like crushed lilies.
Confused like a nightmare in waking hours.

Tears came to Patricia's eyes.

Rachel said, "I feel your emotion and thank you for sharing this. The way you expressed yourself is profound. If you wish, we might meet and talk together at some point."

Patricia wiped a tear from the corner of one eye and then nodded.

"How about after lunch, if that's alright with you?" Rachel asked.

"Yes," Patricia responded.

From my previous discussion with Patricia, I learned something about the source of her feelings, but I'd be the last person to know what to do about them. When she read out her similes, they somehow touched me in a way I couldn't explain.

Rachel then looked at Diana.

Diana smiled and read out,

Hopes like billowing clouds glorifying the sunrise.
Unconditional love is an eternal foothold.
Fear, like a tightrope walker powerless to cross the chasm.

Rachel said, "That's an intriguing mix, of hope and love and fear, each one extremely powerful. I'd love to explore this with you if you would like?"

Diana replied, "That might be helpful."

"May I propose later this afternoon?" Rachel asked. Then, she turned to me and nodded.

I said, "I'm not too sure about this, having little experience with metaphors and similes. And, digging into emotions is not what I normally do. So, I strike out on both counts."

"That's okay," Rachel said. "You are free to share or not."

"What the heck," I said, so read out my three,

No answers to feelings, like they are vacuumed away.
Numb as a bum.
Empty and not even wanting a refill.

When I finished, Barry raised his head backward and rolled his eyes to heaven. He put his elbows on the table, placed his head in his hands and groaned, "At least one is a simile. Numb as a bum. That's good. And, it rhymes."

Rachel ignored Barry and said, "Mack, this is a profound exploration of your emotions. That's excellent. If you would like to explore this or any other aspect of this workshop, then we could meet."

"Sure," I said.

"I'll get back to you to propose a time," she said. Then, she stared at Barry.

He gave three, each one read slowly for dramatic impact, again like he was on a stage. He said, "I am feeling the following."

Confident as Hercules.
Strong as the voice of Fate.
Free as bird on branch, just as ready to fly east as west.

As he finished, Diana spoke up from across the room. "I'm sorry, but I think the last one is already from someone and maybe the first."

Rachel looked at Diana, and gave a slight smile combined with a small, almost imperceptible nod.

"What do you mean?" Barry asked.

Diana said, "I'm sorry, Barry, but it's the old schoolteacher in me. I've spent the last ten years correcting papers. The last quote is from Elizabeth Barrett Browning, I believe."

"Is it?" He asked. "Well, shame on me. You know, when you read so much literature, sometimes that material becomes internalized. I guess that's what happened, although the simile expresses my feelings, and that was the reason for the exercise. And, who's to say that Browning didn't get her idea from someone else, maybe even from me in a previous life." He sat straight in his chair and glared at Diana, as though preparing for war.

Diana lowered her eyebrows, focused on Barry, and didn't speak, and I imagined her using that expression to gain control in a classroom.

Rachel said, "Let's move on. Jade, would you like to share?"

Jade didn't hesitate and read out,

Angry as a lioness in a net.
Lost like a star without a galaxy.
Lonely as shattered porcelain.

Rachel said, "That is beautiful."

"Thank you," Jade said.

"These have exceptional depth, and I'd love to investigate them further with you if you would like?"

"Yeah, that might be good," Jade answered.

It was difficult to perceive how Jade's similes applied to her. They expressed solitude, like *a lost star without a galaxy*. *Shattered porcelain* reflected brokenness. But, these similes had nothing to do with how I perceived Jade. To me she was outgoing, and a strong-willed free spirit. The aspects of anger and loneliness didn't work for me, but that shows how much I know about reading people. Although, my experience in the financial world had taught me that what you see on the exterior is not always what is happening below the surface.

It was remarkable how the other participants seemed to be in touch with their inner world. They seem to have easily identified their feelings and then developed them with metaphors, like Patricia who expressed her confusion and readily associated that to a nightmare in waking hours. That spoke personally to me. It was a mystery how they did this. My three metaphors were pitiful in comparison.

* * *

As we broke for lunch, I was perplexed. Why did I have such difficulty in recognizing my feelings? Did I even have any?

Jade's metaphor of being angry like a caged lion came to my mind. That one struck me. Anger is something I had felt in the past. Over the years it had boiled up in me from time to time.

I thought back to growing up as an only child never knowing my father. My mother died when I was young, and I moved in with my grandmother who kept me fed and clothed, but her interests were soap operas and the senior club down the street with its nights of Bingo and gin rummy. Affection and love were foreign. Many kids are versions of me.

In school, I became an introvert, and science and math were my favorite topics. In the evenings I buried myself in textbooks and enjoyed figuring out solutions to mathematical problems. At the top of my class in these topics, I just got by in other subjects like history, social sciences, and English.

My grandmother encouraged me to play sports, as it meant less supervision during the afternoons. The benefit was that it kept me off the streets and away from gangs. So, I played football, basketball, and baseball, the sports that cycled you through the year. During summers, I made money as a lifeguard.

Of all these, I liked football the best and couldn't wait until the season began. One reason I loved football was that it was a way to release anger. When a runner charged directly at me, it was like two trains meeting head to head. I wished that the opposite team would send a fullback toward me on every play.

Because of my football abilities in high school, I got an athletic scholarship to a large university. There, I put on weight, gained strength, and tackled even harder, yet, I never paused to consider the source of my anger. To use Jade's illustration, it wasn't a lion in a net. It was a lion wanting retribution, but from what?

At the end of my last season, several professional football teams contacted me, but I took a different direction. I played through the final games of the season with an injured knee. Knowing it would take a beating in the pros, I headed off to graduate school to pursue a Master's Degree in Finance.

By that point, I was focused on one thing, to get the degree and get a job. Suppressing emotions had become the norm, and it stayed that way even while managing the mutual fund. But deep down I worried about a volcano ready to erupt.

When Jade read her simile, I related to it. I had never adequately dealt with the angry lion in my soul. In reflecting on what had been read out by the participants, I was touched by several of their metaphors, even those of Barry. They were real poets, for they caused me to consider something more profound.

* * *

Lunch was served at the same circular table as the previous day and Barry took a dominant role, making jokes about similes. He said nothing about Diana's challenge to his work.

At one point he said, "Mack, your work is hilarious."

"What do you mean?" I asked.

"You lack imagination. *Numb as a bum* doesn't make any sense. Do you mean bum like a hobo, and why would a bum feel numb? The logic doesn't work."

"In the conference room, you said it rhymed."

He snickered. "Any third-grade kid can rhyme words. They say things like *See spot run – Let's have fun*, or *Throw the stone - Get the bone*. You can do better than that. Now, you've got potential with your '*Empty and not even wanting a refill*' but it needs fixing. I could rework it a million ways."

"You can have it," I said.

On the first day when he introduced himself, he said he was a teacher in a junior college. I wondered how his students responded to him? While I didn't like him, he was right. I knew little about literary techniques.

The main course at lunch was *chuletas de cordero*, lamb chops cooked with thin slices of garlic. The meal was delicious, and I tried to connect it with a decent simile, but still had difficulty. I considered *Noodles like man food*. That would not make it into a literary journal. *Meat cooked like a book*, would not pass Barry's standards. It just wasn't working.

Similes had zero importance in the financial world. Facts and methodologies are what counted, not ethereal sayings of stars without galaxies and shattered porcelain. It was inconceivable to think that a mutual fund manager would tell investors that "*the fund performed like a sinking boat*". For me, the entire premise of the workshop was suspect.

After lunch, I went to my room, stood by the window and looked out at the turquoise waters in the bay. To the left was the town of Cadaques, spread out along the water, its old church the most prominent structure.

I glanced to my right and noticed movement. Patricia walked down a path and then turned onto the terrace of a small house next to the hotel. Rachel came out from around the corner of the house, shook Patricia's hand, and then gave her a short hug. Rachel motioned toward the terrace, and they disappeared around the corner of the house.

I went to my creaky bed and laid down and thought of Patricia. I admired how she had so willingly shared her feelings with the group.

My feelings were unknown, so what was there to share?

* * *

In my room, I went to the mirror to check out my injuries. One side of my face was still purple, and I looked like I had been in a war zone. My headache was still there. A concussion can take up to ten days to heal, so I still needed to be careful.

When looking at the stitches on my forehead, I remembered the two attackers in the park. It was bewildering why they had come at me like that, and strange that they knew my name. Had I done something to anger them? For six months, I had hardly spoken with anyone, so why would they do this?

It had to be a random attack. Everything happened so fast and I may not have heard them correctly. Maybe my imagination was playing tricks. The only thing not imaginary was the stitches on the side of my face, the purple bruises, and the pain I felt in my ribs, head, and legs.

Jade's metaphor came back to me. Release the angry lion from his cage, and he would get retribution.

I rested on the bed, spending much of my time distinguishing colors, primarily those in the reproduction paintings on the walls.

On one wall was a painting of The Last Supper, a surrealistic portrayal of the disciples, all with bowed heads at a table. Christ is slightly transparent, with his right index finger pointed toward heaven. There was a transparent figure of a man behind him in the sky. Behind the disciples was a bay that looked like the bay of Cadaques.

A painting on another wall was of the back of a woman looking through a window, her elbows resting on the lower window frame. Light blue curtains brought harmony to the blue in the woman's dress, as well as the sea beyond the window. Again, the sea seemed like the bay of Cadaques. I liked that painting, as it portrayed tranquility.

While I picked out colors and details in the paintings, for the life of me, I could not form any similes, and that was frustrating. How could similes and metaphors come so quickly to the others in our workshop, but not to me?

Perhaps there indeed was something in me that was empty, or numb.

Then I noticed the signature of the artist on the painting of the woman by the window. It was by Salvador Dali and dated 1925. I couldn't see the signature on the other painting of the Last Supper but guessed it was also by Dali.

In the New York City Metropolitan Museum of Art, I had seen one of Dali's paintings, of Christ, crucified on a cross suspended in the air. I just wondered why our hotel, the *Casa des los Poetas*, would have reproductions of his paintings?

* * *

I rested for an hour and then went back to the conference room and joined Diana, Barry, and Jade.

When I sat down, Barry laughed and said, "Frankenstein's monster has emerged."

I stared at him without responding. He would have to get used to it.

Rachel and Patricia walked in, and Patricia took her seat, and Rachel stood at the front of the room. Patricia's eyes gazed at the table in front of her like being lost in a trance. Whatever she and Rachel had discussed must have been soul-searching.

Rachel said, "We are attempting to use metaphors to gain deeper insight. You might say, our goal is to think like a poet. What does that mean? To adequately answer that question, we could ask, what is poetry? Most of you have English Literature backgrounds. So, what is poetry?"

"Why is that so important?" Barry asked.

"What do you mean?" Rachel replied.

"Poetry is many things, but fundamentally it is a form of writing. You need to get it right, and that only comes through learning the techniques."

Rachel asked, "In poetry, then, what are the right techniques?"

"Those we are taught in our studies," he replied.

"So, may I ask which techniques are the best ones, for instance, those of Emily Dickinson or those of Dylan Thomas? They had very different styles."

"I prefer Dylan Thomas, so his techniques are the best."

"How did you come to that conclusion?"

"I like his style."

"It sounds like personal preference is the main criteria in determining right techniques versus wrong techniques, rather than using some other standard."

Barry nodded. "That's correct. I believe in the authority of the self, and it's my feelings that dictate reality and nothing else. If I feel something is, then it is."

Rachel paused and then smiled, as though she had discovered something profound about Barry. I wasn't sure what that had to do with poetry.

She said, "Your statement is fascinating, and we might have a lengthy dialogue, but I'd like to move on. But Barry, I am curious about one thing. If you honestly feel that something is true, you would act upon it. Is that correct?"

"Of course."

"If you feel you could fly, would you jump off a cliff?"

"Ah . . .," Barry replied. "I'm not sure I'd ever feel that."

"But, you don't know for sure."

"Nothing is absolute."

"So, can we conclude that reality is different than feelings, although feelings might be real? For instance, in my illustration, the cliff is a reality, whereas your feelings may be something different."

"There is no way of ultimately knowing, for reality is an illusion," he said. "All I feel is that there is no true-truth. Everything is subjective according to each individual's interpretation. And, because each person carries a unique experience, that proves no truth is final or absolute. I don't fully experience anyone else's feelings, but I do sense mine. It's all I have to go on."

"Would you ever consider that there might be an infinite, absolute source of truth outside yourself?" Rachel asked.

Barry stayed still for a moment, and replied, "That's an absurd proposition."

Rachel gave another small almost undiscernible smile. "You stated that as an absolute, but based on what you said about everything being subjective, we might interpret your statement as having little meaning, if any."

It looked like Barry wanted to respond, but instead, he looked down at the table. Their discussion had reached the limits of my understanding of philosophical things, but I had the impression Barry realized that no matter what he said, it would only be interpreted as subjective opinion. In other words, in staying consistent with his beliefs, any statement of fact coming from him would be seen as meaningless by others.

"I need to think about that," he said.

Rachel turned to the participants and said, "Let's move on by going back to the original question. What is poetry?"

I spoke out. "Something that rhymes?"

Barry laughed. "You mean like numb as a bum."

"Why not?" I challenged.

Rachel cut in. "To create rhymes is well known in poetry. But, what exactly is poetry?"

"It's a form of language," Diana said.

"Yes, and what else?" Rachel asked.

"It's concise, yet goes beyond the literal," Patricia answered.

"Excellent," Rachel commended.

Jade said, "It's revelation of elemental truth, done in a newfangled way. It opens and enlightens. For instance, if you say, the yellow flowers are a burst of sun, it gives an insight into the magnificence of flowers."

Rachel laughed. "I like that, to reveal the truth by using newfangled perceptions." She paused, then said, "Poetry has many definitions, so it's not easy to put your finger on it, but let's combine your thoughts and go with that. Poetry can be rhyme or prose. It's a concise form of language that stretches beyond the literal, and with new insights, it reveals truth. I'd like to add that it tests our paradigms."

She went up to the whiteboard and wrote down a condensed version of our input. Then she turned back to the group and said, "We now have a working definition of poetry. If our goal is to perceive like poets, do you have any thoughts on what this means?"

In considering the confined life in my apartment, I said, "Perhaps it's to gain new awareness, like seeing one's situation differently."

Rachel said, "That's a good point. What you are saying is that to think like a poet would enable new insights into one's reality."

"There's that reality word again," Barry said. "There's only one way to see it, and that's through feelings."

"I have a different take on it," Jade said. "Imagine that the ultimate reality is that all is one. In fact, at the end of time, all will morph back into the universal singleness. Therefore, what we see and feel are illusions, for the ultimate state is oneness. To think as a poet would lead to that reality."

"What do you do with feelings of pain, hate, and love?" Rachel asked. "Can you ignore them?"

Jade smiled. "It's not easy. But, one can try."

"My view is different," Diana said. "As a Christian, I believe that God created diversity and therefore we live in a world of complexity. To think like a poet is to see that complexity for what it is."

Barry spoke out. "You don't believe that religious hocus-pocus, do you?"

Diana stared at him with the authority of a school teacher and said, "I do. That belief changed my life."

"It's a children's fairy tale, like believing in Santa Claus," he stated.

Diana stared at him and said, "You might consider which worldview has the best fit for reality. Basing one's life on feelings might be the absolute fairy-tale."

"Reality is what you believe it to be, or to be more precise, it's what you experience it to be." Barry stated.

Diana responded, "I understand feelings, because I have them, but one would be completely lost by operating only on subjective experiences. My belief is that we need outside revelation to make sense of reality."

"So, you know it all." Barry refuted.

"I don't. Life is a mystery, but we can know enough to make some sense of it, that is who we are and our purpose."

"Good for you," Barry stated. "But, I feel you are misguided."

I sat watching the interaction and admired Diana for sticking up for her beliefs. Worldviews and belief systems were never something I explored. My life had been filled with the here and now, of how an oversupply of oil impacts the share price of steel companies.

It seemed that Barry, Jade, and Diana were looking at the world in different ways. In Barry's case, reality was relative, whatever he believed it to be, while dictated by feelings. Jade's view was that 'all-is-one' is the ultimate reality. And Diana thought that a divine being created the world and all its complexity, although she still had questions.

Rachel said, "This is an interesting discussion. My question has to do with perception, that is, thinking like a poet. You have given different perspectives, which can influence how you see. Are there any other thoughts?"

I said, "I've never given much thought to religion or worldviews. Maybe I should. But, doesn't it seem like we can let the people around us take away our ability to think clearly, and therefore we lose our freedom?"

Patricia spoke out and said, "I agree with Mack. Our culture and the beliefs of the people around us have a big influence on our identity. At least that's my experience."

Rachel replied. "I think you are both on to something. The world can form our thinking, how we perceive ourselves, and therefore that may determine what we do or don't do."

That made sense. Something in my background limited me, and of course, my experience with Linette had brought me to a state of indecision.

Rachel said, "Irrespective of worldviews, I am asking you to explore perception, and to use poetry as a means for doing this. So, the assignment this afternoon is to create a poem that meets our working definition of poetry." She pointed to the whiteboard.

Poetry is a concise form of language stretching beyond the literal. With fresh insights, it challenges paradigms and can reveal truth.

Rachel said, "The subject of your poem can be anything, whether an object or experience. Try to test your perceptions. Find a place that works for you, and I'd ask you to be back here in two hours."

As the students got up to leave, Rachel called out. "Diana, would you be willing to spend some time with me?"

Once outside the hotel, we went in different directions. Rachel and Diana took the path leading toward the small house off to one side of the hotel.

I walked up the hill toward the pine tree where I had been the first day. Rachel had given us another ambiguous task, which was not for me.

* * *

It was a warm afternoon with a slight breeze coming off the sea, and the pine tree provided shade from the sun. The assignment was perplexing, to write a poem that met the definition on the whiteboard. It was to test a perception.

I looked down the hill at the bay which opened to the endless sea, a blue expanse covered by shimmering reflections, like a mirror fragmented into a thousand pieces. Then I thought of Patricia's metaphor that the sun is a torch to the soul. I liked that. Being in the sunlight does something to you. It lightens and cleanses.

To my left was the village of Cadaques. Before, I had only seen white buildings and tile roofs. Now, numerous new details emerged. The town was a myriad of shades of whites, browns, and reds. There was little symmetry to the buildings, each one a different size and shape, each planted in a different position.

The sage bushes on the hills were dark and light browns, and I took notice of the details of spiny branches.

Then, I laid on my back and pulled my straw hat down over my face. Looking up through the hat, I noticed pinpricks of tiny light rays coming through the holes between weaves. I concentrated on them, considering how a powerful, bright sun can penetrate dark places. The pinpricks of light made a fascinating design. Still, how do you relate that to anything personal? How can that help solve one's problems? How does that link to a definition written on a whiteboard?

Frustrated, I got up and wandered down the hill and into town and went to the same café bar as before and ordered an *agua con gas*. It came in a cold bottle, condensation droplets running down the label on the side. The server popped the cap on the bottle and poured the water into a chilled glass with a few ice cubes on the bottom, and a slice of yellow lemon floated to the top of the water.

People walked by, some carrying towels heading for the beach. Others strolled into side streets.

On my notepad, I wrote down a couple of lines. It was a futile exercise.

* * *

Back in the conference room, Rachel asked us to read out our poems.

Patricia said,

Two reflections in the mirror,
Competing to dominate the landscape,
A white lace curtain like an elated socialite,
A cracked window, despairing, wounded.

Rachel said, "That's wonderful, a struggle between contrasts, so simply expressed, yet so profound."

I understood it. Patricia told me about her internal conflict. Now, she had described it in a poem by using ordinary objects one would find in a room. There were two images used, one pure and delicate, and the other used and broken. I was awestruck by how she had done it.

Rachel nodded at Diana, who said,

This boat, a soul heartening from sea,
Held by undying winds, uplifting,
To eternal haven

Rachel smiled, and said, "The sea, boats, and winds are things we see and experience every day here in Cadaques, but one would not think to connect them to something higher, as you have so beautifully done. Now, Mack, would you like to read your poem?"

I said, "I don't have a clue in the world if I am doing this right. I borrowed from Diana's metaphor and tried to extend it." I read,

A hundred pinpricks of light penetrating through holes in a straw hat,
attempting to become torches for the soul.
Lemon, ice and agua con gas exploding senses in different ways.

Rachel laughed with joy, and said, "You have combined the external world with the internal. Well done." She looked at Barry.

Barry said,

I am not mine, not lost in me,
Not lost, although I long to be,
Lost as a candle lit at noon
Lost as a snowflake in the sea

Barry smiled and said, "See there. Rhymes work."

Rachel frowned. "I think I've heard something like that poem before."

Diana spoke out. "That's right. It's from Sara Teasdale, although something doesn't sound correct."

Barry laughed. "Mack borrowed from Diana, so I borrowed from another poet. What's the big deal? My version redefines the object in the poem and therefore totally changes the meaning."

"What did you change?" Patricia asked.

"The original was, I am not thine, not lost in thee. My version is modern. I am not mine, nor lost in me. Do you see the difference? It means everything."

"Indeed, it does," Rachel stated. "Let's move on."

Jade read out,

The telephone,
Words transiting,
Over fiber-optics,

Linear back and forth,
Circling sweet talk cajolery,
The obligatory pretense of caring.

Rachel said, "Again, here is an example of using an object that we carry in our pockets and turning it into something deeper. Through Jade's poem, we see a relationship acted out. It touches our emotions, and that goes back to our definition of poetry."

While I understood the poem, if it had anything to do personally with Jade, I didn't understand. I knew nothing about her.

Rachel pointed at the whiteboard. "You see, Jade's poem meets this working definition of poetry. Her poem is concise, stretches beyond the literal, and it reveals elemental truth and reality by using new insights. Thank you for sharing this."

Turning back to the participants, Rachel smiled and said, "That definition is pretty good. Our day has been good, and we have made progress, although we have a ways to go. To end the day, I'd like to read just a few lines from a poem written by someone who sees the world as a poet. This poet expresses the loneliness he experiences because of the unique way he perceives reality. The poem is titled, Alone." She went to a table next to the whiteboard, took a piece of paper and read from it,

From childhood's hour I have not been
As others were; I have not seen
As others saw; I could not bring
My passions from a common spring.
From the same source I have not taken
My sorrow; I could not awaken
My heart to joy at the same tone;
And all I loved, I loved alone.

She held her eyes to the paper, and asked, "Does anyone know who wrote it?"

Diana answered, "Edgar Allan Poe."

"That's correct. Poe is one of the great poets. He was aware of a special ability when he said, *I have not seen as others saw.* Starting tomorrow, that's what we'll be exploring, the ability to see uniquely."

She put the paper back on the table and said, "Tomorrow, please be in front of the hotel at seven in the morning. You are going on a field trip."

* * *

Dinner was a quiet affair out on the terrace. Barry and Jade carried on most of the conversation talking about who was the best travel writer. They threw names back and forth, and there was no agreement.

Patricia and Diana appeared somber, lost in thought, picking at their food and slowly chewing each bite. They declined dessert and said they were going to bed.

They left, and then they stopped at the edge of the terrace, and I caught a sentence or two.

"How was your time with Rachel?"

"Incredible."

"It's like a weight is gone."

"I need time to think."

I didn't get the full conversation as they went into the hotel, but it seemed that they had both gained something special from their meetings with Rachel.

The dessert was *Crema Catalana*, a cream pudding with a caramelized crust on the top. Barry and Jade continued talking, but I ignored them, because I was thinking about poems. Rachel said my poetry was well done, in combining the internal world with the external. I laughed to myself. That was my first real poem if you ever wanted to call it that. Maybe there was hope yet, but I wouldn't bet on it.

After dinner, Jade said, "Would you like to go with us to town?"

Barry looked away.

"No thanks," I said. "I'm tired."

"Frankenstein needs his sleep," Barry said.

I looked him in the eyes and said, "Frankenstein may come after you."

"Ha, ha, that's a good one."

I got up from the table and walked back to my room and went to bed.

It was another restless night, caused by jetlag, the concussion and the intensity of the workshop. I had no problem spending hours facing the stress of the stock markets, but this workshop was different. It was getting to me by playing tricks on the mind. Rather than dreaming about share prices, I faced a penetrating plague of telephones, lost boats at sea, lions in cages and a multitude of other images all mixing.

* * *

Wednesday

At six-fifteen in the morning, I got up and took a quick shower. The field trip sounded like a welcome change, for I wasn't sure I could take another day of introspection. I needed a break.

After a quick breakfast of coffee and a croissant, at seven o'clock I stood in front of the hotel where a minibus waited. Patricia and Diana were already there. Rachel arrived, and shortly after, Jade joined us, her hair wild and uncombed. A few minutes after that, Barry turned up. It seemed like he was missing sleep.

Rachel told us the minibus would take us to Figueres, to the Salvador Dali Museum. Figueres was the town where I had gotten off the fast train from Barcelona.

Rachel said, "The museum officially opens at nine o'clock, but I have connections, and they will let you in early. The hallways are narrow, and the museum gets crowded during the day. To see it without the crowds of people is a better experience for you. I am not coming along. You will have four hours in Figueres, and you are free to spend the entire time in the museum or to walk around the town. Take notes and write down your impressions. The van will pick you up at twelve, and you will be back here at one o'clock for lunch. Then there is another session this afternoon where I will give the next exercise based on your discoveries in the museum."

"Why the art museum?" Barry asked with a groggy voice. "I thought this was a poetry workshop."

"It is not a poetry workshop," Rachel answered. "It's an opportunity to learn to see in a new way."

"So, why are we looking at art?" He asked.

"What's interesting is that Salvador Dali had a different outlook than most people. Art is a perception, and it often reflects a philosophical system.

"What was his philosophy?"

Rachel laughed. "That's an excellent question. He eventually painted as a surrealist, but he was also a cubist. Some would say he was only having fun. All I ask is that you spend a little time with Dali. Look at the colors and images in his art, but also, try to get into his head, if that's even possible." She laughed again. "He had imagination. You'll see what I mean. We can discuss this when we meet this afternoon."

I wondered what we were getting into. Visiting art museums was not my favorite pastime.

Footprint 5: Listen.

There's a lot of difference between listening and hearing.
G. K. Chesterton

Listen to the MUSTN'TS, child,
Listen to the DON'TS
Listen to the SHOULDN'TS
The IMPOSSIBLES, the WONT'S.
From Listen To The MUSTN'TS
Shel Silverstein

The minibus followed the same road as the taxi I had taken from Figueres to Cadaques, first through the hills along the coast, and then it turned west at the coastal town of Rosas. While the road to Figueres was busy, there was no longer a traffic jam like on the previous Sunday morning.

In Figueres, the mini-bus drove through narrow streets and finally came to the side of a large red building. The driver parked the bus and then said to follow him.

We walked along a sizeable pinkish building dotted with hundreds of sculpted golden objects that appeared to be loaves of bread. Along the top edge of the building, were giant white eggs, and between the eggs were golden statues of nude women.

We came to a door, and the driver knocked on it, and a moment later the door was opened by a woman wearing a uniform. The driver and the woman spoke to each other, and then he turned and instructed us to be back at the bus at twelve o'clock.

We entered the museum, and the guard left us on our own.

"So, what now?" Barry asked.

"This is exceptional," Jade said. "Have you ever had an entire museum to yourself? Let's go."

As we walked through the entrance, I saw that we weren't alone. In a courtyard, there was a small group of people, and they were looking at an old car. The car was a Cadillac maybe from the 1940's, and on top of it was a tall and mesmerizing statue of a nude woman with large breasts, and on her head was something like a Roman helmet. Around the patio on the walls were gold statues embedded in enclaves in the walls.

This was a bizarre place, and I had no idea what Dali was trying to express, but it seemed like he was messing with your head.

We went from the courtyard into the building where we faced a large painting that looked like the backside of Venus de Milo.

Diana said, "Hey, it's Abraham Lincoln."

"What are you talking about?" Barry challenged. "It's the rear end of a hot woman."

"No, no," Diana said. "Look at it carefully. It's Abraham Lincoln."

"I see it," said Patricia.

"Me too," Jade remarked. "You just need to squint a bit."

I squinted, and sure enough, Abraham Lincoln's face emerged. "That's pretty neat," I said.

"You're putting me on," Barry challenged. He stood looking at the painting for a minute or two and said, "All I see is the hot chick."

"Let's move on," Jade said.

We walked down a hallway and stopped to look at paintings. Gradually our group broke up, as one by one we became mesmerized with different paintings.

I found it to be a fascinating art exhibition, much different than the Met in New York, where I had been with Linette.

Dali's art was diverse, some scenes realistic, and others downright weird.

I stood in front of one called 'The Spectre of Sex-Appeal', with a beachside scene of a small boy standing and looking at an abstract monster seated by the sea.

Four people came to the painting, and one, who seemed to be a tour guide said, "This is Dali as a boy, dressed as a sailor. Dali described the painting as, 'an instant photo in colors at hand subconscious, surrealist, extravagant, paranoiac, hypnagogic, extra-pictorial, phenomenal, superabundant, super-fine images, of concrete irrationality'. You will notice that this monstrous figure in the painting is soft and hard at the same time, which for Dali symbolized sexuality, Crutches, to Dali, represent death and resurrection."

The group moved on, and I continued looking at the painting, now understanding that Dali portrayed the world in symbols. Then I wondered what it would take to see the world as symbols?

I moseyed from one painting to another, fascinated by them, attempting to figure out if they carried hidden messages. It was impossible to know, so instead of looking for special meaning, I looked at the details of the colors and shapes. Most images were distorted or unnatural in one way or another. Eventually, I found that the paintings strangely affected me. Some felt like an attack, and I began to feel dizzy.

By ten o'clock, the museum became crowded, and I felt claustrophobic. So, I left the museum, walked past a long line of people waiting to get in, and then took a small pedestrian street. There were several art stores along the street selling reproductions of Dali's works. I paused by the window of one of the shops and spent time looking at an image of St. George attacking a dragon.

Next to the image of St. George was this strange photo of Salvador Dali, which was just as surreal as his art. Rachel had laughed when she suggested that we try to get into his head. Was that even possible? It seemed he continually forced you to ask one question. What is real?

It was getting to me, so I continued down the street toward the central part of the Figueres.

After finding an outside café, I sat down and ordered a black coffee and a croissant. Then I took out my notebook and wrote down my impression of the museum.

As I drank my coffee, Jade walked by holding a shopping bag. She saw me and came up to my table.

"Hey," she said.

"Join me, if you want." I motioned toward a chair, and as she sat down, I asked, "Been shopping?"

"Yeah. After traveling light for a month, I could use a bit of clothing. This town has a lot of small stores, and the prices are good."

"So, you scored?"

"Just what I needed. A pair of slacks. There's a blouse in one shop that interests me, so I'm going back."

"How about a coffee?" I proposed.

"Thank you, that would be good."

I ordered a *café con leche* for her and then asked, "How did you find the museum?"

"Fabulous," she said, "but I could only take an hour of it."

"Why's that?"

"I'd go crazy if I stayed in there."

I laughed. "I know what you mean. It's well outside my normal existence."

"Mine too," she said.

I waited a moment, then asked, "What's your normal?"

"You don't want to know."

"Why not?"

"It took me five years to get through university, because I changed my major several times, finally graduating with a degree in English. I graduated three years ago, and then floated." She smiled. "At least my family says I'm floating."

"Floating?"

"It means I'm avoiding the life-path they have chosen for me."

"Have you been working?"

"Not according to my parents. I've been managing a coffeeshop."

"No kidding."

"Yeah, I love it," she said.

"Five years at university sounds expensive."

"Crazy expensive, but that's the least of my worries."

"Why's that?"

"My parents funded everything, and they continue to do so."

"That sounds like a good deal," I remarked.

"Not really. It's better to be independent. I hardly talk to my parents, and when I do there are always demands." Her face became drawn.

I asked, "What's the situation with your parents?"

"What do you mean?"

"How and where do they live, and all of that?"

"My mother and father divorced when I was six, and each has been through two marriages since then. Stepbrothers and stepsisters appeared along the way, and I now have a collection of mothers and fathers and siblings. It's confusing and much of the time overflowing with drama. Somewhere along the way, it's like they left me at the side of the road. But, whenever I try to do something with my life, the entire clan magically gets involved, and whatever I do is never good enough. It a life of do's and don'ts, should's and should not's. Eventually, one feels powerless, and you only want to rebel, but I'm getting too old for that."

"Wow, that's tough," I said, thinking again of the *constraint* word.

"My parents are wealthy. They have homes and condos all over the place. Social events and travel consume their lives, but they rarely call to ask how I am doing."

I looked away, not knowing how to respond. Then, when reflecting on our previous day's session, I said, "I think this provides background to your poem, the *sweet talk* and *obligatory pretense of caring.*"

"You remembered."

"Yes, I'm good at remembering, but terrible at metaphors and poetry."

She smiled. "I won't comment."

"Please don't."

Her shoulders relaxed, and she said, "Don't worry about it. Rachel keeps saying the important thing is to think like a poet."

"Do you know what she means by that?"

"I guess she means that you get into a certain state of mind. What do you think?"

"She's been clear. She says it's to see the world differently, to discern things as they are. Maybe that's something to apply to your family."

"I'm not sure about that. There's too much complexity."

"If not, what then?"

"I've got the credit card." She smiled.

"How does that make you feel?"

"Dependency isn't fun."

"Is that how you want to live the rest of your life?"

She hesitated, and said, "If I told you what I'd like to do, you'd laugh."

"Try me."

"I'd like to own a coffeeshop. With the one I managed, the revenue tripled in one year, and the owners made a good profit. If I had my own shop, it would do the same."

"Then why not do it?"

"My parents would be horrified. It's too low class."

That didn't click with me. I said, "My background is business and finance. The basic business principle is that if you see a need in the market, you fulfill it. That's an honorable thing."

"Try and tell my parents. For them, the honorable thing is to trust their lives to financial advisors, stock brokers, accountants, and lawyers."

"I understand," I said, not wanting to tell her that I had managed an investment fund. I knew what she was talking about, for I had looked out for the portfolios of people like her parents.

I changed the conversation. "I see that you and Barry seem to hang out. How do you see that going?"

She grinned. "Jealous?"

I smiled back. "Outrageously so."

She laughed.

"I've got enough problems of my own to be jealous of anything."

She looked at the coffee cup in front of her and said, "He's not my type, although he doesn't get the message. Our only similarity is that we are two broken souls, but also quite different. Barry is floundering because he can't find meaning in anything but his feelings, and I think he sees that as shaky ground to stand on. I'm just trying to think like a poet to get a new perspective on things. Two broken souls. That's pretty weird isn't it?"

"Not really," I stated, knowing our group had more than two broken souls. Diana, Patricia and I needed to be included. Diana was fighting a demon from the loss of her husband. Patricia was suffering from being used, to use her terminology. And, I had confined myself to a cave.

Jade stood up and said, "Thanks for the coffee."

"Thanks for the conversation," I said.

She looked at me, and said, "I never thought I could share that with anyone, especially a threatening looking guy whose face looks like it went through a meat grinder."

"That's funny."

"What happened?" She asked.

"Baseball bat."

"Do you play baseball for real?"

"I never said that."

"You're full of mystery. Unfortunately, I've got to run. I need to get to the clothing shop. But, I'm curious to hear your story. How about we meet another time?"

"Sure."

"See you at the bus at twelve," she said."

I nodded.

Jade took her bag, started to walk away, and then turned back to me. She said, "I like you, Mack. You listen. That helped me."

I watched her walk away. She wasn't the confident young woman I had imagined. She carried personal baggage, and it was breaking her, just like me.

What she said struck me, that I listened. That was a powerful word. **Listen**. Sometimes we talk too much, not hearing others, not trying to understand.

I learned something by merely paying attention. I learned something about Jade and a truth about myself. Like her, I had become powerless, but what was the source?

* * *

Barry was ten minutes late getting back to the bus. Patricia, Diana, and Jade stared at him with steely eyes. Barry laughed it off, and said, "I had to savor my experience." He slightly slurred his words.

I wasn't sure what he was talking about but felt uncomfortable the way he disregarded the women. I said, "The time was twelve o'clock to be at the bus. We should have left without you."

He snickered. "You don't belong here." He pushed past everyone and took a seat at the back of the minibus.

As the bus started to roll, Patricia said, "That museum was amazing. Salvador Dali's work was beyond creative. He was in another realm. Did you see the thing with Marilyn Monroe? I don't know what you would call it, a statue, or an optical illusion?"

On the floor in one room was a large object of red lips and several feet away was a huge nose. Behind those objects, two paintings hung on the wall. On the opposite side of the room, you looked through a round glass, and the objects and paintings merged into the image of a woman's face. "It was pretty crazy," I said.

"More than crazy," Jade added. "Dali's creativity blew my mind. He pushed reality in all directions."

"What is reality?" Barry asked.

Jade countered, and said, "Oh, come on Barry, let's not get into one of your philosophical elucidations."

"Reality is what I want it to be, but I didn't find the museum to be special. It's evident that Salvador Dali used art to provoke people, only for commercial purposes. He could have sold ice to Eskimos. Just throw in a few colors, form them into a weird shape and bingo, someone spends a fortune to buy it."

"You're a spoil-sport," Jade claimed. "So, what did you do this morning."

"I took a quick walk through the museum, but it didn't excite me, so ambled around Figueres. Eventually, I found a bar with a bunch of old guys playing card games, and drinking brandy and beer."

"So, is that how you spent your morning, with brandy and beer?" Jade asked.

"Yeah, I got more out of that than visiting childish drawings stuck to walls."

"Good for you," Jade said.

After that nobody talked, and I wondered about Barry. I didn't like his attitude and didn't like the negative comments he made toward me and others in the class. I had an uneasy feeling about the guy. Who was he? He said he was a teacher of English Literature at a junior college in California and it seems that a teacher would be interested in visiting museums and discovering new things.

If school started in September, why wasn't he back in California teaching a class? Barry said he was also a travel writer. Perhaps the visit to the bar would provide material for an article, but why forsake the visit to such an iconic museum? He was a mystery.

The other mystery was Rachel. Here, in a remote village in the Costa Brava, was an intelligent and beautiful woman giving courses. She had a good thing going because marketing teams flew to Spain to attend her class. Who was she and how did she get here?

The course baffled me. Much of the time, we were on our own, whereas Rachel's time with us was minimal. She came into the room, spent a few minutes giving an assignment, and then left. Then a few hours later we came back together, and she asked each student to share what they had written, and she made a comment or two. She had not given any presentations, although she had spent time one on one with Patricia and Diana.

She used the small house next to the hotel, and a couple of times I had seen her walking into the center of the town. The article in the newspaper said she had a Ph.D., but in what?

As far as achieving results from this workshop, I had my doubts. The newspaper article said the course released those marketing guys from constraints, and that's what motivated me to attend. That's because over the past months, I had been in a bottomless pit and needed help. Despite all the hype about poetry, this course wasn't doing any good.

My mind circled back to a previous question. Was this a scam? Was it like those seminars given by pseudo-cult speakers who give motivational speeches on personal success, and health and wealth?

The ride back gave me time to reflect on my state of mind. The poetry workshop wasn't helping, and I didn't see hope in anything else. Did that mean I had given up on life?

It's odd how we chose our life paths. In university, I was on an athletic scholarship and lived in a house off-campus, shared with a few other football players. They were all highly academic, so that rubbed off on me. We didn't go to drinking parties. We studied, worked out and focused on football.

The man who owned the house was an alumnus of the university who had made a fortune in the stock market. He was retired and occasionally came by to hang out with us, and to give advice. I never had a father, and he became something like a father to me, the first male role model I ever had.

He encouraged me to go to graduate school, and when finished with school, he was the one who got me the job as a junior trader for a mutual fund company on Wall Street. Then he died, which was devastating for me. At that point, my career was on a track, and I hunkered down and applied myself and over the next ten years achieved success.

But despite the so-called success, I was lonely. And, then I met Linette.

I met her at a party at the end of the year. My firm got together with other investment companies, and we celebrated a year of successful results. Stock prices were up, and our clients' portfolios had done well. We received exceptional bonuses.

Linette attended the party, and I never understood how she was invited. She unquestionably didn't work for an investment company. The only certainty was her beauty and how quickly she became the center of attention. At the party, they gave me an award, an absurdly large bonus check, for managing the top performing mutual fund for the year. After receiving the award, Linette migrated to me like a prospector finding the motherlode.

She gave me her telephone number, and I gave her mine, and then for a week, I agonized about calling her. What would she see in this big, homely looking ex-linebacker? Then, she called me.

After that, it was a whirlwind of dinners and visits to cultural events, and parties with the political and financial elite of New York. Linette opened my world and brought energy to my life. She was spontaneous, and I was reserved. She loved designer clothing and extravagant jewelry, whereas, I preferred jeans and t-shirts. We were at opposite ends of the pole, but she cast a spell on me impossible to escape.

One Friday evening she said, "Let's get married."

By then, I was captivated by her spontaneity and deeply in love. I wanted to spend the rest of my life with her. On a whim, we flew to Las Vegas, got married and had an incredibly wild weekend.

Then the fast life continued and eventually I understood that Linette had one prevailing talent. She knew how to spend money. The unwritten clause in our marriage contract was that I made money and she spent it.

But then, the universe crashed.

* * *

We had lunch after returning from the Dali Museum, and the afternoon session started. I desired to be somewhere else. The visit to the museum had been an attack on the senses. Still feeling the aftereffects of the beating in the park, I needed sleep and hoped that Rachel would not take too long before dismissing us on an assignment. I planned to lie down in the shade of the pine tree on the hill and take a nap.

Instead of going to the front of the room, Rachel stood off in the corner behind me. It felt odd.

She said, "For many people, a visit to the Dali Museum can be mind-bending. Dali plays not only with your senses but also your perspective. He was part of the surrealist movement after the 1920's. According to art historians, that movement aimed to achieve a super-reality by resolving contradictions between dream and reality."

"That's a joke," Barry said, turning to the back of the room to face Rachel.

"Why do you say that?" She asked.

"How can you resolve contradictions, when there aren't any?"

"Can you expand on that?"

"Dream and so-called reality are delusions, for what is real?

"Then, it seems you are siding with the surrealists."

"Feelings supersede everything. That is the reality. That's the truth."

"That's an interesting statement. You stated it as an absolute as though it is true, but I understand you don't believe in truth," Rachel said.

"Only feelings are truth."

"Then, on what do you base this truth?"

"There is no other plausible explanation for truth, for every belief is a leap of faith. Feelings are all that's left."

"Oh. I see, but perhaps you are closer to the surrealists than you think. You might say, they attempted to fuse hallucination and certainty into a new paradigm. It may be that by using feelings as a base for truth, it employs the same dynamic."

"I need to think about that," he said.

I had a difficult time keeping up with that argument. What is real is the bottom line, meaning revenue minus costs equals profit. In what fictional realm were these people living?

Rachel continued. "The Surrealist movement expanded from art into political thought. This movement said it was imperative to free up imagination. To accomplish this, people needed liberation from suppressive and outdated social structures. This thinking influenced the French student revolts in 1968, and their slogan was, *All power to the imagination*. Barry, I sense you have extended this to, *All power to feelings*."

"That's right, and that's why I couldn't spend more than ten minutes in that museum. My feelings were not validated, and I found a bar where they were."

My head hurt as I listened to this exchange. I suspected Barry didn't like the museum because he couldn't see Abraham Lincoln's face in the nude lady painting. That hurt his pouty ego. Maybe by basing his life only on feelings, it limited his ability to see in new ways. In that painting, he saw a "hot chick", and nothing more.

Rachel said, "Let me go back to Dali, which leads to our exercise. You have seen that many of his paintings are fanciful scenes with bizarre creatures formed from everyday objects. It was an attempt to allow the unconscious to express itself. Just for today, I'm asking you to push your poetry in that direction. Try to go outside the box. Perhaps use one of Dali's paintings as a base for expanding your perception."

She walked to the front of the room, and said, "You may have noticed that I started by standing at the back of the room, rather than where you had become accustomed to seeing me. Because of this, you may have felt uneasiness. It is a simple illustration but shows what happens when our routines are interrupted."

She moved to the side of the room next to the window. "The assignment is to push your thinking, to even go illogical or abstract if you need to. For instance, you might try to express unrelated combinations of colors, objects, and feelings. I'm not asking you to become a Surrealist and will state upfront that my worldview comes from a very different source."

"What's your worldview?" Barry asked.

"That would be a distraction and is not the purpose of this exercise. I prefer that each of you examines your worldview, that is, to define what you believe, and then to test it. See if you can drive yourself to the logic of your presuppositions."

"You're cheating," Barry said.

"Not really. The objective is to explore your perceptions, not mine. I don't want to sidetrack you. Let's stay with our goal to think like a poet and not deviate. This afternoon, expand your imagination. What you write may be revealing and even shocking, as you have seen in many of Dali's images. Let's see how it works. Use the rest of the day for this, and we will meet back here tomorrow morning.

"You didn't tell us your worldview," Barry said.

"Discover your own," Rachel stated.

My head pounded. This exercise seemed ridiculous. To expand your imagination meant that one might transit from the world of the logical to the illogical. I was most comfortable when living in tight logic. But, that raised a doubt. During the past months, was it possible my thinking failed me by not being broad enough, by not allowing imagination to have a place?

As I stood up, Rachel said, "Mack, we had discussed spending time together. Would you be free now?"

My body ached for a nap, but I said, "Yes."

* * *

Rachel and I walked outside the hotel and down a path to the house beside the hotel. After turning the corner, there was a table with four large chairs. The chairs were wooden, and they had turquoise cushions faded by the sun. A large umbrella provided shade.

Rachel pointed to one of the chairs and said, "Please take a seat. Can I get you something to drink? Tea, lemonade, water?"

"Tea would be nice," I said.

"With lemon or milk?"

Not being a tea drinker, I wasn't sure, so said, "Lemon."

Rachel disappeared into the house, and I looked at the view, Cadaques to the left and the bay stretching out in front. It was a warm early September day, and a breeze transported the faint salty smell of the sea.

93

The sun sparkled on the water, like glittering jewelry. It made me feel sleepy.

Then, I wondered what Rachel wanted to talk about, and it made me nervous. Even though she was older than me, being alone with women always made me nervous.

She arrived carrying a tray with a teapot, two porcelain cups, a small silver bowl with sugar cubes, and a small plate with slices of lemon. There was also a bowl of cookies.

"I'll let it steep before pouring it," she said. "Please have a biscuit."

"A biscuit?"

She laughed. "British for a cookie."

"It's a beautiful view," I said, noticing how the blue of the sea complemented her blue eyes.

"I'm lucky to live here," she said.

"Is this your house?" I asked.

"Yes."

"It's quite a setting. How long have you been here?"

"Two years. It all started with an inheritance which included this house, the hotel, and a building with a couple of apartments and an art gallery." Rachel smiled. "After taking full responsibility for these assets, we were faced with a challenge. They needed to pay for themselves."

"I'm a business guy, so I totally understand. Is that the reason for starting the poetry workshops?"

"Not really. The workshops began as an experiment, and then they took off. The revenue from them is a benefit, but I started them because of personal interests."

"To help people?" I questioned.

"Yes. People benefit from them."

"Do you give the workshops all year long?"

"No. Six months out of the year, with two workshops per month. They are intensive, so one must avoid burnout. I balance this with writing and painting."

"Painting? Like Dali?"

She laughed. "Not like Dali. I'm not a Surrealist. My view of the world is different. But, let's not talk about me. Tell me about you. What motivated you to take the workshop?"

I took a breath, not knowing how much to tell her. "In New York, I saw the write-up in the newspaper about your workshop and thought it might be interesting."

"My goodness. That came out on Saturday morning, and you were here on Sunday. It sounds impulsive."

"It was."

"Why?"

"I saw the part about learning to think in new ways and about being released from constraints. Perhaps I need a new way of looking at things."

"And, you were able to step away from work and come here?"

"That's right."

"May I ask what you do?"

I hesitated. "I'm an independent stock trader." I was reluctant to tell her about sitting in front of computer screens for sixteen to eighteen hours a day.

"So, you have some independence?"

"Yes and no."

"What do you mean by that?" She asked.

"I suppose I can step away from my work at any time, even travel the world, but, to be honest, it's like . . . ah, . . like Jade's metaphor about a lion in a cage. Only I'm not sure what the cage is or how to get out of it."

Rachel looked out at the sea like she often did, her face smooth, her golden-brown hair reflecting a ray of sunlight that came through a small crack in the cloth of the umbrella.

She poured the tea into the two cups and offered me a slice of lemon. She put a slice of lemon in her drink, so I did the same.

"Sugar?" She asked.

"No, thank you,"

She lifted her cup and took a small sip, then turned to me and said, "Have you considered what keeps you from getting out?"

"Out?"

"Out of the cage?"

"Oh." I took a breath. "Stuff happened."

"Would you talk about it?"

I shook my head, no.

"That's okay," she said. "May I ask about your accident."

"My accident?"

"It seems you were injured, at least the bruises and stitches are a giveaway."

"My face encountered a baseball bat."

Her eyebrows raised in curiosity. "What happened?"

"Just one of those things."

"It looks like more than a thing."

"I was in the wrong place at the wrong time. Thugs in Central Park have been beating up homeless people, and they surprised me on an isolated bench."

"But, you said you trade stocks. Are you homeless?"

"No, but they may have mistaken me for one. I had on old shorts and a ratty t-shirt."

"Did you go to the police?"

"A policeman accompanied me to a clinic where I got the stitches, and he made out a report."

"So, how does this make you feel?"

"Feel?"

"Yes, you must be feeling something."

"Maybe anger, but mostly I feel numb."

"Numb?"

"Yeah, the same numbness I've felt for months."

"And, why is that?"

"I'd rather not talk about it. I thought we were here to talk about poetry."

She smiled. "Not poetry. To think like a poet, at least in some ways."

"I'm still not sure I'm getting it. What is it exactly?"

"It's to discern in a new way, to challenge the logic of presuppositions, a helpful thing for everyone to do."

"Maybe I won't achieve that."

"Maybe you won't. Some don't. At least we can try."

"In the article in the newspaper, it said you have degrees from Oxford University. May I ask the subject?"

"I have a Master's Degree in English Literature. It was quite an honor to go there because that's where J.R.R. Tolkien and C.S. Lewis taught."

"If I remember correctly, the article said you also have a Ph.D."

"That's correct. In Psychology."

"You mean you're a Psychologist?"

"Yes. I'm a member of the British Psychological Society."

My heart dropped. Here I was with a shrink."

* * *

The muscles in my neck tightened. I had assumed Rachel was a literary geek. Knowing she was a psychologist put me on my guard. I didn't want anyone digging around in my head, for it was a complicated place. I needed to shift the conversation from me to something else.

I said, "I'm confused. How do you mix poetry with psychology, if that's what you're doing?"

She smiled. "It's possible, and a way to combine two of my interests. When I was young, I read a lot and took an interest in the classics. I particularly liked mystery stories, especially those that dealt with human thinking. Therefore, literature and psychology became two interests and I was fortunate to be able to combine them."

"How's that?" I asked.

"Have you ever heard of Metaphor Psychology?"

"Sounds weird."

"It's not. It's a type of psychotherapy that emerged from the work of Carl Jung. Without getting too technical, it uses metaphor as a method to help people symbolically express their experiences. Psychologists practicing this form of therapy believe it is a tool to involve both the conscious and unconscious to explore personal meaning."

"That sounds technical."

Rachel smiled. "I guess so. Usually, this is one-on-one therapy, but I began to experiment, first by expanding beyond metaphors and into a broader poetic construct. Then, I saw that it could achieve rapid results when done in groups. This is different than traditional therapy. It's more a way of helping people by using poetic methods as a means of exploration."

"You mean to think outside the box."

"That's correct. And, this goes beyond psychotherapy in that anyone can gain benefits."

"Psychotherapy?" There was no way we were getting into a counseling session.

"The workshops are relevant to anyone wanting to gain new insights into their lives, or perhaps see a problem in a new way, or use their imagination to become more creative. The applications are wide-ranging."

"You should get a Nobel Prize," I joked.

She laughed with a warm smile, and said, "That's a stretch. My method would need to be scientifically studied before it became a recognized treatment. I'm sure some Freudians might think I'm a kook. That's okay. For now, I'm happy that people benefit from the workshops. Poetry and art are my passions, and the workshops pay the bills. I enjoy giving them if they don't become all-consuming. I think I've found a balance, but I must say that I'm tired by the end of October when the workshops stop."

"So, because it's a workshop and not a therapy session, you could conclude that I'm not a mental patient."

She smiled. "You are simply the participant in a workshop, and I am simply the facilitator."

I took a deep breath and tried to relax, but it was still unsettling to think she might be analyzing me. I decided to be hyper-cautious around her over the following three days.

"Where is your art gallery?" I asked.

"I'll show you if you'd like."

I quickly agreed, knowing this would get me away from an encounter dangerously close to becoming therapy.

* * *

We made our way toward town, and that relieved the tension. Still, I was uneasy wondering what Rachel had discovered. It was unnerving to think that someone might be exploring my blank inner world.

We walked along the narrow road next to the sea, which sometimes passed by rocky shorelines and at others went by small sandy beaches. We turned left past the café bar where I had previously been, and then turned left at a sign pointing to the *Museu Cadaques*. Two minutes later, we came to a building close to the museum. Outside was a sign saying, *Galería de Los Poetas*.

I said, "It seems you have a common branding with the 'poets' name on both the hotel and the gallery." It was an effort to keep the conversation on neutral ground.

She smiled with a look that told me she knew my game. "Maybe we ran out of creativity," she said.

"I like it," I commented.

We walked into the first room in the gallery. It was large, and on the walls were a mix of paintings of different styles. I said, "After spending this morning in the Dali Museum, I thought it would take a long time before wanting to visit another art exhibition."

"Look around," Rachel said. "Spend as much time as you want. Now, if you'll excuse me, I need to check on something."

Rachel went into another room, and I saw movement, and she spoke with someone. It was the younger woman I had seen walking with her, the one who had looked at me with penetrating eyes. They walked up a set of stairs at the end of the room.

I turned, and on one wall were several paintings. Upon a closer look, they were more like short, hand-written poems with colorful, artistic images painted around them. I went to one and read it,

Walk still on tempestuous seas,
Roiled by Tramontana winds,
Tides of Fate leading to
Unintended places.

Around the poem were abstract brush strokes that may have been a churning ocean, but with softer and lighter strokes on the upper right of the canvas.

Another painting was about love.

Love eternal,
Unexplained,
Even in the disappearance,
The Glow
That never dies.

This one had soft rose brush strokes surrounding the poem. I had to think about both poems and their meanings. The flowing signature at the bottom of the painting was R. Eden, which could only mean Dr. Rachel Eden. I stopped and wondered what she implied by these poems. What did she mean by *Tramontana winds* and *love eternal*? What had motivated her to write these poems?

Indeed, she was not only a psychologist facilitating workshops. She was also a poet.

Romantic piano music came from somewhere in the gallery, soft and slow, with minor notes. It seemed like a recording was playing, but then it stopped, and several times a line of music was replayed. Someone was practicing a piece of classical music.

Several rooms branched off from the main room. In one room was an artist's workshop with a large easel standing in the middle of the room. On a table next to the easel were tubes of oil paint, a painter's pallet, and paint brushes. The easel held a canvas with a painting in progress of an almost lifelike young girl with innocent piercing blue eyes. She held a red flower to her lips and a blue sea was in the background. There was something serene yet mystical about the painting.

A. Eden

I turned and entered another room, and my eye immediately went to a large painting on the wall. Not knowing much about art, I thought it looked something like the Impressionists' paintings I had seen in the Metropolitan Art Museum in New York City, with surrealism mixed in. But, what did I know about art?

It was large, rectangular and the main image in the painting was of a slender woman walking along a beach. The sea behind her was of solid blue. I had never seen a blue that intense. The sky was in lighter tones with clouds reminiscent of some I had seen on paintings in the Dali museum. The woman walked barefoot on light grayish blue sand, leaving light footprints behind her.

A. Eden

She wore what seemed to be a cotton dress, transparent in several places revealing her legs. Her body was long and feminine. The artist portrayed the woman in a fluid, relaxed step. A small label was stuck on the wall below the painting giving its title, *Poetic Sea*.

I stood back from the painting and admired how it was a mix of a realistic person walking in a mystical world. For some strange unknown reason, the peaceful flow of the young woman caused me to relax, and I felt a serenity I had not had in months, maybe even years. This painting had a different effect on me than all the art in the Dali Museum. This one played with my senses in a very different way. It created an odd sensation, and I decided I had to take it back to New York.

The signature on the painting was, A. Eden and I assumed the artist must be related to Rachel Eden.

I had the impression that I recognized the young woman in the painting. Then, I heard a voice behind me, but being focused on the artwork, I didn't catch the words. "Excuse me?" I asked.

The person behind me said, "Do you like it?"

Without turning back, I stared at the painting and said, "Very much so. Do you know the artist?"

There was a laugh. "I do."

I turned, expecting to see Rachel and was caught by surprise. It was the tall young woman who had been walking with Rachel in the village, who had looked at me with penetrating eyes. They were the same eyes as on the painting on the easel in the other room, of the young girl. I was uncertain how long she had been standing there.

"The painting is beautiful," I said.

She commented, "It reflects a mood, like contemplating endless worlds."

I said, "For me, it creates a calmness, and I like the peaceful flowing movement in the main character there." I pointed at the young woman in the painting.

"Are you an art connoisseur?" She asked.

I chuckled. "I visited the Met in New York City a few times, and some galleries in the city, but I am a complete novice. All I know is that I like this one. Can you tell me the price?"

She hesitated and with a soft voice said, "It is eight thousand Euros."

I did a quick calculation of the exchange rate. That was much less than most of the paintings Linette had chosen. I said, "I'll take it."

She gave out a small breath, and said, "It's my favorite. It clings to you like satin fingers. I set a high price almost hoping that no one would buy it."

"I'm sorry," I said. "Perhaps there is another one?"

"No. No. This is an art gallery. Everything is for sale."

"Then, you have a buyer. I promise it will have a good home and be very much enjoyed." I looked at the painting and then at her and remarked, "I see a resemblance."

"I hope so," she said. "It's an auto portrait."

"You painted that?"

She laughed. "Don't say it like that. My art fills this room."

"I see that. And, the young girl on the easel. Is that you?"

"Yes. It's a painting modeled after a photo taken when I was young."

"It's wonderful," I said, wishing I could describe paintings like the art experts at the Metropolitan Art Museum.

"I like how it's progressing, but it still needs work, like a recipe missing an ingredient," she said.

I didn't know what more it needed and would have taken it as it is. I turned back to the painting on the wall, of the woman walking by the sea, and said, "I have never seen a blue like that. It's powerful."

"You noticed," she said.

"How can one not notice."

"That blue is special and very expensive. A French artist, Jacques Majorelle created it. He patented the formula and trademarked the name, Majorelle Blue. It is intense, unlike any other, a deep vastness with no horizon."

I asked, "I was at the Salvador Dali Museum today and learned about symbolism in paintings. What were you thinking of when you painted this?"

She smiled. "Many things, but mainly about choices. The future is mysterious and unknown. There are many options in life, but one must decide on a direction, and then have the courage to take the first step."

"I see that."

I looked around the room. It had paintings in a similar style. The subjects were people at coffee-bars, the beach, small fishing boats in the harbor and old houses. Some used Majorelle blue.

"They are all very nice," I said, knowing there were better words to describe them. "And, please add the painting of the poem in the other room, of *walking on tempestuous seas.* I like it, and it will give a nice memory of my time here."

"Rachel will appreciate hearing that," she said.

"I find her to be exceptional," I commented.

The young woman smiled, and said, "I do, too."

We went to the main room, and I paid for the two paintings with my credit card. Then, I wrote down my name and address."

"I'll ship them tomorrow," she said."

"And, please let me know when you are ready to sell the self portrait of you as a young girl, the young poetic sea."

She smiled and said, "That's an interesting title, although the painting may never be finished. I'm attached to that one and it would almost be like giving my soul to someone. It would need to be the right person. I'll let you know."

"Thank you. Please do think of me." I asked, "Were you playing the piano?"

"I was. Every artist needs a diversion. Mine is music and writing poetry."

"What was the piece you were playing?"

"Tchaikovsky's Romance in F minor. His works are like sunlight on an iridescent sea."

When she said it, I noticed her eyes brightening and I searched for a simile or metaphor to describe it. I couldn't. It's strange how one gets impressions of people. In her, I sensed something found in her art, an appealing mystery.

She walked with me outside the gallery, and we shook hands. When I got to the end of the street, I turned, and she was still standing by the front door of the gallery. She smiled and waved.

When I arrived at the road by the sea, I realized I had forgotten to ask her name, which meant that I had purchased a painting without knowing the name of the artist.

Then I had an odd sensation, wanting to go back and linger in the gallery.

It's weird how something can assault you in a second, unknowing and unexpected. Maybe the visit to the Dali Museum had impacted me, or perhaps it was this zany poetry workshop, but I was unsettled. Something was causing me to do abnormal things, acting on impulse.

It started with the attack in the park and then finding a newspaper article that spoke about being free from constraints. Then, it was far out of the ordinary to hop on an airplane and fly to Spain. That act was utterly contrary to my routines and calculated existence.

The most unexplained impulse was spending thousands of dollars on a painting. I did it in a blink. Was something or someone messing with my head in a way I didn't want? Was it Rachel? The time with her on her terrace had raised my defenses, but now, meeting this young woman had left me vulnerable.

The contact with this young artist touched me in a way that was difficult to describe. The piano music. Her elegant movements and poetic descriptions. It was fascinating to hear her speak of a painting as clinging like satin fingers, or Tchaikovsky's music as sunlight on an iridescent sea. It was fascinating.

Was I becoming unhinged? I couldn't answer that question but understood that I needed to get control of myself. I needed a game-plan to make it through the next two and a half days of this workshop if even possible. Should I immediately head to Barcelona and get on an airplane and go back to my apartment in New York City? That thought was depressing, and I was still not physically whole and needed more time to recover. Travel was out of the question.

I decided on a simple plan, to relax over the next days and try not to do anything impulsive. It was evident that I wasn't any good at this metaphor business, but Rachel said it was a form of therapy. The workshop led toward a new way of seeing one's world. But, if you didn't have a spot of talent, was it worth trying?

* * *

Thursday

In the morning I felt better. For the first time, I slept through the night without taking painkillers. It was a sign the concussion was healing.

After breakfast, I went to the conference room. The assignment was to use Dali's art to expand our imagination, whatever that meant?

To complete an assignment based on imagination was foreign to me. In math classes at school, there were right and wrong answers. In the investment world, decisions came from logic and reason, and not from fancy.

Rachel's assignments were obscure and undefined. How weird was it to identify colors and emotions, and then elaborate on them with similes? This latest assignment of imagination was even more ambiguous.

I had written something but had no idea if it met expectations. Without a doubt, Barry would mock it.

Was my nervousness irrational? Was it based on my fear of rejection? Why should I be concerned about a handful of literary elites that I would never see again? I needed perspective.

In New York, I had managed a mutual fund and worked with some of the most influential people on Wall Street. I had meals with them, gone to parties and had developed a network of contacts. I knew lawyers and publishers and politicians, many having invested in my fund. Before leaving my company, I had gained a position of importance.

Now, I was in a meeting room in a modest hotel in a small village in Spain and worried about rejection by a few people who had studied Shakespeare. And, I had learned that my fellow participants had issues of their own. Why should their acceptance matter? Maybe my fear came from something profound, a life-long hang-up that was never adequately reconciled. The workshop might be bringing that to the surface. Had Linette's rejection broken me beyond repair?

I just needed to make it through the day.

Rachel came in and made a short introduction, again reminding us that the purpose of the workshop was not poetic correctness, but rather to see in a new way.

That was not yet a reality for me.

Then, she spoke of the assignment, to expand our imagination and think out of the box. But, she also said that after the next session, the workshop would take a new direction. Specifically, we would explore the concept of wisdom, as a way of developing perception. She then asked us to share our poems.

Patricia started. She said, "One painting in the Dali Museum was titled, *Soft Self-Portrait with Grilled Bacon*, which is a rather funny title. The subject is Dali's melting face supported by crutches. Somehow, I related to that painting, for I know how it feels when your soul melts away. Here goes."

She took a deep breath and waited for a moment, as though she had doubts about reading it. Then she peered at the paper in front of her and eventually shared her poem.

Amorphous irony,
Title on the pedestal,
Bacon breakfast of,
Flayed skin,
A familiar impression,

Like evaporation on burning desert sand,
In need of salvation,
Reminiscent of Michelangelo's
Sistine Chapel,
In search of supporting crutches.

There was a moment of silence and then some nods around the room.

"Wonderful," Rachel said with a smile. "Indeed, it's been theorized that Dali associated that self-portrait with Michelangelo's representation of himself on the Last Judgment fresco on the altar wall in the Sistine Chapel. Michelangelo portrayed himself as a hopeless, empty skin only saved from hell by Saint Bartholomew's hand."

Patricia bowed her head while looking down at her poem. Her cheeks reddened, and apparently, she was experiencing something somber, because the lines on her face tightened.

Rachel said, "Now and then it is possible to feel like that, like soulless skin in need of support."

"More than you know," Patricia stated.

Everyone in the room went still, not knowing if anything should be said. I admired Patricia for being open like that in front of everyone. Was the poetry workshop working on her like it was for me?

Diana went next, and she said, "Dali seemed to have an interest in watches, bending and twisting them. Those paintings caused me to think about eternity and time, and how it is difficult to grasp it fully from a limited perspective."

Then, she read her poem.

A watch slithering over hot stone,
Liquefying,
To a place,
Where time and beyond time exist
Side by side,
Immortal, invisible,

God only wise,
Not directly answering the question,
Why?
But knowing answers,
To be revealed.

"Thank you," Rachel said. "It is remarkable how you brought two very different sources together, Dali's watch with the old Welsh hymn *Immortal, Invisible* by Walter Chambers Smith. Your poem then traverses to beyond time where certain answers can only come from an only wise God. We may get into that later in this workshop. That's a perfect use of imagination."

Diana sighed and then laughed. "I'm not sure it's the best of poetry and certainly would not know what grade to give if one of my students wrote it, but it comes from the heart. Do you think I should rework it?"

Rachel smiled. "Don't rewrite it. Our purpose is not poetic correctness. It is to see the world with insight. It looks like you've achieved that by equating Dali's watches to eternity by thinking of a divine being who exists beyond time. Well done. Keep imagining."

Rachel looked at me and said, "Mack, how about you?"

I hesitated and said, "The paintings in the Dali Museum were fascinating, but eventually I had to leave the place to clear my head. Being there felt like an attack. It's like Dali lived in a dimension far beyond my daily life. It's difficult to figure him out. His stuff seems to be symbolic. If you aren't trained to spot this, then you get confused, and it gets to your head."

"In what way?" Rachel asked.

"You suggested that we could use Dali's art to step outside the box and even see beyond the normal. For me, it felt more like falling into the unknown. I became disoriented and needed to step away."

"I know the feeling," Rachel stated. "Did you write anything?"

I chuckled and said, "Not very good. Just some thoughts jotted in my notebook." I read from it.

Being in the Dali Museum was like living a thousand hallucinations. It played mind tricks that I eventually couldn't handle, so I walked outside into the warm sunshine and stopped by a shop selling posters of Dali's paintings. Behind the window was a reproduction called 'The Lance of Chivalry' portraying Saint George killing a dragon with a long lance. A nude woman is in the background, so one deducts that Saint George is saving the woman or protecting her honor. I don't know where it came from, but for some unknown reason, it triggered the thought that vows of empty words are lances bringing ache. I left the art shop, went down the street and found an outside café, sat down and had difficulty remembering the assignment, for my thoughts were going everywhere.

The moment I finished, Barry started clapping. He jeered and said, "Not much of a poem, but at least you got a metaphor in there, *a thousand hallucinations*. Maybe there's hope yet."

Rachel said, "Actually there are two analogies. Besides the one that Barry recognized, there's another that vows of empty words are lances bringing ache. I'm familiar with that painting, and I like how you symbolically equated the lance to vows. That's way outside the box. It is very well done."

If I was honest, I hadn't done anything special, but maybe this was a breakthrough. In spite of my buried feelings, I was able to express something about Linette.

Barry asked, "What's the inspiration for your poem if you even want to call it that?"

"A progression of events," I replied.

"What events?" Barry asked."

"I'd rather not say."

"Oh, come on," Barry challenged."

"It's okay," Rachel said. "No one is compelled to share anything they don't want to. Please remember that the purpose of this workshop is not to share life stories. Barry, do you have a poem?"

"You bet. It's titled, *Who Cares?*"

Catalonia card games
Morning Brandy drinkers
What are their names?
Who cares?
Poetry workshops
And a Poetic Wannabe
What's his name?
Who cares?

The room went silent. Barry was speaking of me. I think he was harboring resentment because I had called him Larry. Anger rose up in me, and I wanted his head on a platter. It was the same emotion I felt in my university football days. All week Barry had been riding me. He was seated five feet away, and with one quick movement, I could be pounding his egotistical face into oblivion. At least I was feeling emotions.

Sure, he was about my height and muscular. I was one second away from punching him when I heard Rachel's calm voice.

"Barry, your poem is an attempt to achieve the assignment, that is, to push beyond boundaries, although you might have gone farther. It reflects cynical hopelessness, but may I ask something? Do you perceive the logical conclusion of taking that outlook?"

"What do you mean?" Barry asked.

"People have names. You have asked if that matters, which is either a seeking of meaning or a philosophical position that there is no meaning. So, how do you prescribe meaning to anything, not only to the names of people?"

Her words were like a silver spike. I was more like a junkyard dog wanting to sink my canines into his leg.

Barry said, "I already told you, it boils down that the only meaning is my feelings. All else is irrelevant."

"Therefore, even though your poem attests that nothing matters, in effect it does, at least to you in a limited, temporal sort of way."

"Well, yes and no."

I was fed up with Barry's vain, narcissistic feelings.

Rachel let a few seconds tick by and then said, "Your yes and no indicates an inconsistency."

"I guess, but consistency isn't important. My belief is that truth changes because feelings change, so just live with it."

"If that's your basic presupposition, we can ask several questions, but let me ask you one. Does your faith limit you?"

"Faith? What do you mean by that?"

"Beliefs are based on faith. In your case, it appears you base your faith on a belief that your feelings are the only origin for truth. So, I'm wondering what it is like to consistently ground your existence on that? You may find that your faith system may limit your life because feelings are volatile and can take you anywhere, often to a place of cynicism and fear."

I was different than Barry, running from my feelings rather than building my life on them. My rejection of feelings had led to a state of impassiveness.

Barry replied, "Volatile feelings are prevalent, and they lead to cynicism and fear along with other emotions, but like I said, just live with it because there's not much else to pin your hat on."

Rachel said, "In light of that, I would bring you back to the assignment, which was to perceive outside the box. Many people get caught up in mind-boxes that are difficult to escape. That not only limits their imagination but also their perspective of reality."

"I don't know what you're talking about," he responded.

"You might want to consider it," she said. "And, I'm glad to continue dialoguing on this if it is helpful."

Barry stayed quiet. Rachel had challenged him in a way I never could, yet, during their interchange, I felt she was speaking directly to me when she talked about getting caught up in mind-boxes that are difficult to escape. That cut to the core. It was the essence of my struggle. My chains were not the computer screens or my apartment. They were my suppression of feelings and an inability to face reality.

As far as faith-systems, the other participants seemed to base their lives on something. I admired Barry for at least having the guts to vocalize his egocentric belief, although it appeared to have made him unhappy. Patricia lived according to the values of the general culture, and I suppose you could call that a belief system. She admitted that it had left her feeling objectified and worthless. Jade believed that all is one. Diana had made her faith obvious. What was mine?

Rachel turned to Jade and said, "Would you like to share?"

Jade said, "I was intrigued by a painting titled *Galatea of the Spheres*. It is of the face of Gala, Dali's wife, broken up into small balls."

Rachel nodded and said, "That painting comes from Dali's nuclear mysticism period. Please go ahead."

Jade recited her poem.

To love is illusion,
To be is deception,
To create is ruse.
For what defines me,
If I am nothing more than fragments?
Minute sub-atomic balls,
Spinning, uniting, breaking apart,
Missing connotation.
An incomprehension,
Of infinite configurations.

"Thank you," Rachel said. "That's an extraordinary insight. Science and the theories of disintegration impassioned Salvador Dali. Gala's face is made up of spheres, and you get the feeling they could fly apart, and of course, it is uncertain how those balls will reconfigure, if at all. So, I see how you come to the incomprehension of infinite configurations."

Jade said, "The question is how one finds their identity if everything is nothing more than an arrangement of colorful detached balls?"

Diana spoke from across the room and said, "May I say something?"

Rachel nodded.

Diana said, "Jade's question is interesting. I don't want to criticize, but if the universe originates from an impersonal beginning, like with matter or energy, and therefore, all is one, then there is a problem. With that assumption, such feelings as love, identity, and self-satisfaction are nothing more than illusions, for they don't reflect the underlying impersonal-ness of being. Her logic is correct."

"That's right," Rachel stated.

Diana continued, "There is an alternative."

"What's that?" Jade asked.

"You might consider a different beginning originating from a personal God, where we are created in his image. That's what gives us our identity," Diana said. "At least, that's what I believe."

"I'll stick with the impersonal," Jade answered. "My existence best fits that. If you knew how my family treats me, then you would understand."

I knew where Jade was coming from because of what she had told me about herself. She came from a wealthy family that didn't take a real interest in her. To use her term, she was caught between the cracks, like a pawn, only there to be moved around by the family. She had to meet certain expectations of how to act, and where to work, and who to marry.

Barry spoke up. "This is getting heavy. What does it have to do with our assignment, to think outside the box?"

Rachel smiled. "Jade went far outside the box, for her poem touched on the fundamental dilemma of humankind. It is the question of how we define ourselves."

"That's easy," Barry said. "As I said before, meaning and truth originate from my feelings, nothing more."

"But, Jade's question is what do you do if those feelings are an illusion? Ultimately the material world breaks down, including our bodies, as depicted in Dali's painting. So, even feelings are temporal. They mean nothing in the expanse of time, as Diana has pointed out. In addition to feelings, any thoughts, ideas, or human actions are meaningless deceptions, for they are nothing more than perpetually shifting sand."

"But, I don't feel that way," Barry stated.

"That seems to be a contradiction. We just concluded that feelings are temporal, and consequently your feelings have no meaning."

"They do to me."

Diana spoke up and said, "Barry, be honest with yourself. Your feelings are meaningless unless you can reference yourself to a greater standard, one that doesn't disintegrate over time. Rather than sand, one needs a solid rock."

"There is no higher standard than me," Barry said.

"But that's temporal, for you won't last forever."

"That's true, but that's the only conclusion to finding meaning in the universe."

Diana said, "Then you must admit that you have a predicament, for, based on your reasoning, everything is ultimately meaningless, including yourself and your feelings."

"Okay, maybe," Barry admitted.

"And everyone else is meaningless, perhaps only objects to be used to validate your feelings," Diana added.

"I already knew that," he confirmed.

"Which then means that relationships are meaningless."

"I guess," he said.

"Which leads us back to the conclusion that feelings are meaningless, and your life has absolutely no value," Diana stated.

"I don't have an answer to that."

"Then why not do what Rachel is asking. Try to think outside the box to look for answers. Why not imagine something different?"

"I don't know," he said, looking down. "You sound like a know-it-all."

Diana shook her head. "Far from that. Many things I don't know, particularly some things about God, but at least I look for answers. What keeps you from doing the same?"

Jade intently watched the interchange between Barry and Diana. Jade said, "Me neither. I don't have answers, knowing my identity is nothing more than an arrangement of impersonal atoms, at least as demonstrated by my family."

I understood Jade, but I didn't know about Barry. I knew he didn't like me, and I disliked him. It made me feel good to see Rachel and Diana questioning him while being glad they didn't do that to me.

Rachel had raised hard questions about faith. As I looked around the room, my attention went to Diana. She was the only one that seemed to have meaningful answers, for she believed in a higher being. At the same time, she carried hurt because of the loss of her husband, and fears about whether she could love another man. And, underneath it was her question of how God could let this happen? She wasn't a know-it-all, as Barry had claimed.

I didn't have answers for Diana, nor did I have a clue about the meaning of meaning. It was beyond me, but Jade's take on Dali's nuclear mysticism opened some dark thoughts.

Fundamentally, did it matter if I made another dollar on the stock market? Did it matter if I reconciled with Linette if that was even possible? I wanted her back, but the possibility of that one was bleak. My conclusion was that the two thugs in the park should have finished me off.

Barry's poem was right on. Who cares?

But, can someone consistently live with that belief? At some point, it seems that people will care about something. How could that caring come from the impersonal unless programmed into humans through evolution? If that's the case, then any feelings of caring are just an illusion if the underlying reality is impersonal, as Diana had reasoned.

That was a scary thought. Maybe I needed to talk with Diana.

This poetry workshop was taking me to new places. It raised questions of worldview and identity, but could it release me from my cage?

I wasn't sure.

Footprint 6: Put reality on the table.

Reality is a question
of realizing how real
the world is already.
            Allen Ginsberg

L unch was a quiet affair, five people seated around a table, each person staring into their private universe.

I left the table before dessert was served and headed to town for a walk, knowing I needed to be back in the conference room in an hour.

Walking on the road along the shoreline was pleasant, a needed break from the weighty philosophical interchange during our last session. The sea was a deep ultramarine blue, bright and intense, like an inverted sky. It wasn't quite like the Majorelle blue in the Poetic Sea painting, but something similar.

The artist who did the painting had called that blue, "a vastness with no horizon." Today I could see the horizon where the sea met the sky, a straight line contrasting an azure sky with the darker sea. I wondered how the young woman would describe this. What was her first name? A. Eden. What did the 'A' stand for? I decided to go to the gallery to find out.

Most shops were closed because of afternoon siesta time, although the restaurants were still going strong with people eating their lunches at outside tables. The sun was bright, and I was glad to have the straw hat.

I turned into the small plaza and went past the café bar where I had sat with Diana, and then made my way to the *Galería de Los Poetas*.

At the gallery, the door was closed, and I tried to open it, but it was locked. Then I noticed a sign on the door. It was closed from one P.M. to five P.M.

Disappointed, I turned away. While I wanted to know the name of the young woman, there was something else that attracted me to the gallery. I was intrigued by her, the graceful movements of her hands and by the way she described things. She was mysterious, and I was curious to find out more.

I walked back to the hotel, determined to return to the gallery and find out her name. For now, I would call her by the name of the painting, Poetic Sea.

In the conference room, the participants took their places with no one saying anything, like exhaustion had taken away our energy. It felt as though each person was dealing with something interior, not wanting to be disturbed.

A million thoughts raced through my mind, of colors, of Linette, of Cadaques, of Rachel, of my stoic life in New York and Poetic Sea, a confusion of images circling.

I dreaded the afternoon session and wanted to go to my room and sleep.

Rachel entered the room and said, "We have accomplished quite a bit since Monday, but there is more to be achieved. Our goal is to see in a new way, and I'd like to link that to the subtitle of my recent book, *An insight into the mystery of wisdom*. Let me ask a simple question. What is wisdom? Would anyone have an answer."

I spoke up. "A couple of days ago you said it was the ability of true discernment or something like that."

"That is close. I said there were several definitions and one is, the power of true and just discernment. Would anyone have another definition or add to this one?"

Patricia said, "Could it be the ability to understand the true intentions of others? For instance, if they tell you one thing and their motivations are something different, like if someone says, 'I love you,' when in fact, their words are a manipulation."

That deepened my understanding of Patricia, for she had told me about being rejected. I identified with that.

"Yes, that's a good insight," Rachel said. "Does anyone else have any thoughts on wisdom?"

"I have a different take," Barry said. "Wisdom is to know oneself as the truth, which is the basis for the entire creation. In other words, wisdom means a person achieves self-awareness."

Rachel paused and said, "Thank you for that input. That's linked to an ancient idea. *Know thyself*, was inscribed on the Temple of Apollo at Delphi, and the Greeks may have gotten that idea from the Egyptians at the Temple of Luxor. Socrates built on this when he said; *the unexamined life is not worth living.* But, I think you have gone a bit farther than their intent. The Greeks seemed to be emphasizing introspection, whereas your definition is a different realization, which is, you are the truth. When you know that you obtain wisdom?"

"That's right," Barry agreed.

"Are there any other thoughts on wisdom?"

Jade spoke up. "I think it's when a person gains an understanding of the nature of the universe, which ultimately leads to the complete freedom from suffering."

"How could this lead to freedom from suffering?" Rachel asked.

"It goes back to Dali's painting of Gala. If you understand the true nature of reality, that all is one, then suffering is an illusion. When you come to a state of fully living this, one can overcome suffering." She laughed. "At least that's the concept, but I continue to suffer. Maybe I'll get there someday."

Rachel smiled. "I suppose we could get sidetracked into a discussion of the illusion of suffering and love and any other human emotion or feeling, but let's not. What you shared is indeed one viewpoint on wisdom which is lived by many people. Are there any other thoughts?"

I had a quick idea and said, "Wisdom is knowledge and problem-solving. It's getting it right."

"Interesting," Rachel said. "Is knowledge the same as wisdom?"

"I suppose there is a difference," I said.

Rachel said, "In psychology, there are various definitions of wisdom. Some psychologists see it as applied knowledge. Others see it as the ability to deal with contradictions, or even the ability to assess the consequences of an action. In these views, wisdom originates from individuals and their cognitive thinking. Are there any other thoughts?"

Diana spoke up. "Excuse me, but let me fall back on my spiritual belief if that's okay?"

"Go ahead," Rachel said.

"In Judeo-Christian thinking, wisdom is seen as one of the highest virtues. God gives wisdom. It comes from him."

"But, you have not answered the question of what wisdom is?"

Diana hesitated, as though she was thinking while doubting herself. She said, "God is wisdom."

"Oh, come on," Barry said. "Wisdom is abstract and can't be a person."

Rachel turned to Barry and said, "I'd like to give space for ideas. What Diana said is one view of wisdom. In fact, in ancient times, wisdom was personified. In Mesopotamia, there was a god of wisdom. In Islamic belief, it says that God gives wisdom to whom he wills. In Greece, particularly in the Gnostic religion, wisdom was a personified woman. So, in these cases, wisdom is seen as coming from a higher being outside ourselves. This concept is foreign to many people in the modern world."

"How can that be?" Barry asked.

Diana asserted, "If you conclude that God is the supreme being, then he sees things as they are. Therefore, in making decisions you can act on your own, or you can ask him for insight."

"You do it your way, and I'll do it mine," he said.

Rachel said, "I think we've explored this enough. Perhaps I can make one further comment and then we can move on to the next exercise. It's interesting that the Book of Proverbs in the Bible consists of quite a few chapters of wisdom sayings, and these are teeming with metaphors and similes. These were a way of amplifying a truth. Here is one example."

Those who trust in their riches will fall,
but the righteous will thrive like a green leaf.

"That's a beautiful illustration to think of thriving like a green leaf, and the righteous have it rather than those who trust in their riches."

That struck me. I had achieved wealth, but I couldn't say I was thriving.

"Here is another," Rachel said,

The fruit of the righteous is a tree of life,
and the one who is wise saves lives.

"In this wonderful metaphor, the righteous is a tree of life, and it is thought-provoking to consider that a wise person saves lives, versus the destruction of lives by people who lack wisdom."

That hit me. In my self-imposed misery over the past months, I had done nothing to help anyone let alone save lives.

Rachel said, "Here's another,"

Like a gold ring in a pig's snout,
so is a beautiful woman who lacks discretion.

"Wonderful," Barry cried out. "I like that illustration."

"Then, you might consider this," Rachel said.

Like vinegar to the teeth and smoke to the eyes,
So is the lazy one to those who send him.

Barry sulked.

I smiled. I would never mess with Rachel.

Rachel continued. "You see, these allegories are wonderful ways of teaching deeper truths. They are tools used to teach wisdom."

She paused a moment and looked out at the sea as she sometimes did, as though gathering her thoughts and considering the best way to move forward.

Rachel said, "We have seen that there are different ways of approaching wisdom depending on one's worldview. For now, let's confine our tactic to one dictionary definition, the power of true and just discernment. And, we will use metaphors and similes as our tool for doing this."

She looked around the room, then said, "I'd like you to reflect on the greatest challenge in your life. Some of you have already addressed personal questions through the metaphors you shared. I'd ask you to dig deeper to look at your greatest personal challenge. Look at it in detail, at the colors and shapes, for lack of a better description. **Put reality on the table**. That's not always easy to do. Try to gain a deeper insight into your greater challenge. Think outside the box. Use your imagination. If possible, refine it to its essence. And then gain further understanding by using similes and metaphors to describe it."

"So, how do you discern things as they are?" Jade asked.

"That's the essential question," Rachel replied. "All of us see through a prism, through our worldview. We must ask if our worldview is adequate to enable true discernment? What do you think?"

Rachel was going in a direction I didn't understand. "What do you mean by a prism?' I asked.

"It's your composite set of beliefs through which you see the world. All people define themselves by reference points. These are the values they have picked up during their lives. It's the do's and don'ts taught by their parents. It's the truths taught by their teachers and religious leaders. It's the things learned from friends, what is considered cool by one's culture at any point in time. These get mixed in with a person's experience and thinking, and it comes out as a belief system or ideology. Call it a prism for lack of a better term, but you could also use worldview."

I didn't see the connection between this and wisdom, and what did this have to do with the constraints I was feeling? "I don't get it," I stated.

Rachel paused and looked at me. "All I'm saying is that your prism influences how you discern, and it may hinder you from correctly discerning. The result is that one's actions may not lead to the best outcome."

Jade said, "Obviously, people are diverse, so it's normal that they would see the world differently. We should embrace that diversity."

Rachel turned to Jade and said, "You just expressed a belief, which is, diversity is a positive value. If consistently applied, would that lead to a true perspective of how the world is?"

"I'm not sure what you mean," Jade stated.

"In holding your worldview, have you ever asked if diversity is always a good thing? Or, are there limits to diversity and what are they? And, who sets the limits and on what basis? In asking these questions, does it lead to realizations about your belief system?"

"I'll think about it," Jade replied.

Rachel smiled. "To think is one component of wisdom, so you are on a good track."

Rachel paused, looked around the room, and said, "I'd like to refer back to that quote from Socrates about the unexamined life. Our next exercise is an opportunity to do that. Give your greatest challenge some thought. Try and look at it from every angle. More than that consider how your worldview is helping you face that challenge. Then try and express that challenge with a metaphor or poem, to expand your perspective on it. We will meet back here tomorrow morning."

We broke for the day, and Rachel walked over to me. She smiled and said, "I understand you did more than visit the gallery yesterday. You bought something."

I smiled back. "I did a little shopping." I had become the king of impulse buying.

"It seemed to be more than a little. We are grateful for your purchase."

"And, I'm grateful for the paintings. I didn't know you were a poet."

"For many years I've dabbled in it. As I told you, I have a degree in English Literature. When these workshops finish in the fall, I devote myself to writing."

"I liked the poem, to *Walk still on tempestuous seas*. It will be a good memory of my time here, although I'm not sure what the poem means. What are Tramontana winds?"

"During winter in the Costa Brava, a violent wind comes out of the north, and it can last for days. It rattles everything. Some people say it drives them crazy. It is called the Tramontana Wind. The seas become turbulent, and the fishermen don't go out in their boats."

"What about the rest of the poem?" I asked. "What does it mean?"

She smiled. "We might talk sometime. I've seen that you also bought another painting."

"Poetic Sea?"

"Yes."

"I like the movement of the young woman and its mystery. The blue is powerful."

"The Majorelle Blue?" She asked.

"Yes, I guess that's what she called it."

"If you noticed, that color appears in her other paintings, but it usually isn't used to paint the sea. In your painting, it gives the sea a special effect."

"It's strange, but I bought the painting without even knowing the painter's name."

Rachel smiled, and said, "It's Alena. She's my daughter."

"Your daughter? I should have guessed. There's a resemblance." I was excellent at spotting details in financial statements but was oblivious to people. I laughed. "Now, I have a name to attach to the painting."

"Indeed. What are you going to do with the paintings?"

"Both will be hung in the living room of my apartment in New York. I'll have to juggle some other paintings around."

"So, are you a collector?"

"I'm not a collector, but just dabble in it, to use your word." What could I say? It was Linette who had bought the paintings, and Linette wasn't a connoisseur of art. She visited galleries only for the attention she received from the owners and her socialite friends. She purchased paintings because of recommendations from gallery salespeople, not that she knew anything about art.

Rachel changed the conversation. "Have you identified your greatest challenge?"

"I think so, but I'm not sure."

"Maybe I can give a little hint. Often challenges come in layers. People face a problem, and they think it is huge, and it very well might be. But, behind it, there are other factors to consider, and sometimes these are not apparent. Therefore, one must dig below the surface. By dealing with those unknown primary factors, it makes it easier to face the perceived biggest challenge."

"That's an interesting insight," I said. At the beginning of the week, I had assumed my biggest challenge was Linette. Then, I thought it was the limitations I had put on myself. Now, I wondered if it was something else.

"Perhaps we could talk about it if you wish?" She offered.

Here we go again. I wasn't ready for a shrink to pry inside my head. "Let me think about it."

"Please feel free. But, may I ask you something else. On Friday night, could you join Alena and me for a drink at my house? It's to show our appreciation for the purchase of our art."

"Thank you. That's very nice of you." I liked the idea of seeing Alena.

"Then, let's say five o'clock. That's early, but I know you will have your final group dinner at seven-thirty or eight."

"Thank you," I repeated.

"We will see you then," Rachel said. She turned and walked out of the room.

The room was empty, and I sat and reflected on what Rachel said, that our most significant challenges can be concealed. What we believe to be a foremost problem might be masking something more profound. I supposed my major issue was Linette, for she was like a disease that had no cure. She reappeared in my thoughts no matter how much I tried to repress her. The hours spent at my computer buying and selling shares in companies was a way to divert my mind away from her, but Linette was a nightmare that didn't go away. Maybe I didn't want her to go away, and that was the problem. To dig through these layers was not a pleasant thought.

* * *

Rachel's advice to look below the surface was obvious. We become convinced one thing is the cause of a problem when it is only the symptom.

Honestly, I knew my biggest challenge. For sure, Linette was a problem, but was that true? When I peeled Linette away, there was something else eating away. It was more substantial than her. It was something originating from childhood, and it impacted everything.

In putting reality on the table, my greatest issue was not something external. It was internal. My most debilitating problem was rejection and the pain resulting from it.

When a father is non-existent, and a mother disappears because of death, that emptiness can make a child feel unwanted. A neglectful grandmother incapable of showing love is another form of rejection. My childhood triggered doubts and questions, and often I had wondered what I had done wrong? I blamed myself for what happened. The thought patterns formed during youth are not easy to erase.

In growing up, the world was uncertain, never knowing who would reject me next. I became a shy, insular kid who retreated into math lessons. With math, at least I had control. The subjective world of imagination only increased uncertainty.

Playing sports was the only redemptive activity that balanced me, for it caused me to interact with others. After university, when running my mutual fund, I achieved success and acceptance from others. But, Linette came along, and her rejection was a final destructive blow.

Rejection was the core of my distress over the past months, and that had forced me to hunker down in a lonely apartment. I had withdrawn from the world to the point where I wasn't doing any good for myself or anyone else.

That fact was now on the table, but what should I do about it? How do I keep this debilitating fear from ruining my life?

We had two hours before the evening dinner, so instead of going to my room, I took a walk on the road that wound up the hill to my pine tree. It provided an excellent place to be alone.

As I came around a bend, I saw Patricia sitting on a large rock, her head held in her hands. Her back and chest were heaving up and down. I wondered if I should turn around and go back to the hotel, but then she saw me, raised her hand and gave a feeble wave.

I approached her and asked, "Are you alright?"

"I've been better," she replied. Her eyes were red, and tears ran down her face.

Dealing with emotions was not my strength. "Can I do something?"

She gave a slight smile. "No. I don't think so."

"Is it the workshop?" I asked.

"Yes, and no. The workshop raises hurts from the past."

"Like a biting wasp," I proclaimed.

She laughed. "You're getting good with metaphors."

"Are you saying that snobbish literary magazines will start to feature my poems?"

"Well, maybe not that good, but stay with it."

"Do you know your challenge?" I asked.

"I think so." She paused and took a deep breath. "When Rachel said that most people are living by a culture, that struck home, for I have been doing this without even thinking about it."

"What do you mean?"

"Ever since high school, I've tried to do what the world expected, wearing the right clothing, using the right jargon and intonation of voice, living by the mores promoted by Hollywood, liberation, feminism, self, and I could go on."

"Mores? What's that?"

"Morals."

"Oh."

"Yeah," she said. "But, some things just don't work."

"Why?" I asked.

"I guess I did what everyone else did for acceptance, but I suppose love was what I wanted."

The discussion was getting heavy. People didn't share these kinds of things with me. I lived in a world of numbers and algorithms and trading strategies. "How's that?" I asked, not knowing what to say.

"I told you before that my relationships have not gone well. In the end, I felt like a discarded object, and it's painful."

I hesitated and said, "I know."

"What do you mean?" Patricia asked.

"I'd prefer not to talk about it, but I went through something like that, probably not the same as you, but I understand what you are saying. The pain is unbearable, and difficult to face."

"Is that your biggest challenge?" She asked.

"I thought so, but I suspect there is something unrecognized behind it, like another layer to the greatest challenge. How about you?"

"I think I need to be more discerning, not only with relationships but with the values the world is feeding me. Perhaps that's my biggest challenge, to see through those values."

"Is that what has caused your writer's block."

She looked at me with sad eyes, sunlight reflecting off her auburn hair. "I'm stuck, and it isn't writer's block. The novel is finished, yet I don't have the confidence to push it forward. I'm scared, have doubts, and that leads to gridlock."

What could I say about overcoming doubts? To make a diversion from her emotional state, I asked, "What's the story in your novel?"

She shook her head, as though not wanting to talk about it, then eventually said, "It's a humorous quest about a young woman searching for her roots. She encounters quirky people along the way, while a snarky old aunt is the antagonist."

"What's an antagonist?"

A small smile appeared as she stated, "You really don't know literature."

"A complete novice."

She took a breath and said, "An antagonist is the villain that tries to stop the hero from moving forward. Anyway, the main character in my story jumps around the country, going from one crazy situation to another, and things get worse and worse, in a funny way, and finally, there is a hilarious ending. One of my creative writing teachers read it and loved it saying it should be a candidate for the yearly American Book Awards."

Patricia's face brightened as she talked about her book. I couldn't see her writing humor, at least not in her current psychological state. "Then why not move forward with it?" I asked.

"Depression, burnout, lack of confidence, you name it."

"Do you have any contacts in the publishing industry?"

"Not really."

I thought about it. Patricia needed assistance. "What if you had someone to make an introduction? Would that help?"

"I suppose, but who would do that?"

"Let me think about it. I can't make promises, but I may have an idea."

"Why not? I'm stuck for solutions, so am open to anything."

"Okay, I'll talk with you tomorrow."

She started to get up from where she was sitting, so I reached across and offered my hand. She took it, and I pulled her up."

"You're strong," she said.

"An old football player."

"And one who plays baseball. Are you feeling better from your injuries?"

"I had a concussion. The headaches are going away."

"You look improved since Monday."

"More handsome?"

"I didn't mean it like that," she smiled.

"Don't worry. I've never been a poster boy, but you might consider doing a new sketch."

She smiled, and said, "You're a kind person. Thank you for listening."

Kind? How do you respond to that? If she only knew the deep-down anger I carried, so buried I was afraid to express it.

We walked together back toward the hotel, and I knew my afternoon was a failure. I didn't come close to understanding how to deal with my supreme challenge, let alone write a metaphor or poem about it.

* * *

Back in my room, I thought about Patricia and what she said. We had similarities, not only about hurtful relationships and rejection but also about blindly going along with the culture.

That described me. When I examined the path of my life, I identified two forces at play. First was a kind of hidden logic that moved me from one thing to the next. Because of success in sports, a university offered me a scholarship. Because I excelled at math, I got a job at an investment company. Had I given adequate thought to what I truly wanted to do? Not really.

Running parallel to these life events was something more profound. It was the social expectations that Patricia had described. The world gets us to believe something is true, yet that can be a lie based on perverse, destructive values. That becomes the norm and we end up reasoning like the world, acting like the world, and even smelling like the world.

Rachel had talked about this on our first day of the workshop, when she generalized two kinds of people, those who blindly live by a culture, and those who walk with wisdom. My experience was different than Patricia's, but we were both living by a culture. I was determined to break from this. In addition, I was determined to not let the rejection of others become a devastating power that brought me to my knees. But how?

With that reality on the table, I didn't know where I was headed once back in New York City, other than going back to play my stock trading game on the computer. Making things worse, I felt I was good for nothing, at least in helping anyone or advancing anything positive in the world. For the past months, I had been caught up with just one person. Myself.

Patricia needed help, and I thought of an idea. There was a six-hour time difference between Spain and New York, so I looked through the contacts on my telephone and made a call. It was to Jim Bennett, a publishing friend of mine. He ran a large publishing company headquartered in New York City.

I had his cell phone number, so didn't need to fight through his administrative assistant.

He answered on the third ring. "Hello, this is Jim Bennett."

"Hey, Jim, this is Mack McQuaid."

"Mack. You came back from the dead. Where have you been?"

"Keeping a low profile."

"It broke my heart when you left the mutual fund. Their performance is not the same. I've had to diversify, and I'm not sure I'm making the right decisions."

"I'm sorry about that, but I was facing serious burnout and needed time off." I wasn't aware of how much he knew about Linette.

"I understand. This lifestyle can get to you. How can I help you?"

"You could help me with a writer. It's someone I came across here in Spain."

"In Spain. What are you doing there?"

"Attending a poetry workshop."

"What? You've gone off the deep end."

"More than you know. Anyway, the writer's name is Patricia Younger. She has a Master's Degree in Creative Writing and has just written her first novel. Can you look at it?"

"Have you read it?"

"Of course not. What good would that do? You're the expert, so I came to you. I need an opinion on the book as fast as possible."

"That's not the way it works in the publishing industry."

"What do you mean?" I asked.

"If you deal with large publishers, first you need to find an agent. Then, the book goes through a lengthy review process, and it's eventually signed off by a committee. That can take months. Established writers are first in line. The reality is that there are slim chances of your friend's book being taken by us. I have to put that out there."

"She can't wait months."

"I'm sorry, but that's the way it works."

"Not always," I stated. "You're the top guy. This writer has got a lot going for her. In this poetry workshop, she writes brilliant stuff."

"And, what about you. Could you send me your poetry?" He laughed.

"Forget it. You'd croak." He said he was not sure about his investment decisions and I had an idea. "What about a trade?"

"What's that?"

"You said you diversified your portfolio and you have doubts. What if I looked at your portfolio and gave some independent advice. The trade is that you make a quick review of Patricia's book."

Jim went quiet for a minute, then said, "That sounds interesting. I've got nothing planned for the weekend, so I could look at it."

"The deal is that you don't hand it off to one of your editors."

"Okay. I agree."

"Next week when I'm back in New York, I'll analyze your portfolio."

"Sounds good to me. Have Patricia send me her book."

Jim gave me his email address, and we hung up.

In life, it isn't always what you know, but rather who you know. It's also how to package a deal.

I left my room, went looking for Patricia, and found her on the terrace next to the hotel restaurant. She had just been served a cup of tea.

I walked up to her, smiled, and said, "Do you have your book with you?"

"My book?" She asked.

"The one you wrote. Do you have an electronic version?"

"Yes, on my laptop."

"Would you like a publisher to take a look at it?"

"Of course. Why do you ask?"

"Because I hope you can get over your writer's block that isn't writer's block. Someone has agreed to review your book."

"What are you talking about?"

"Not what, but who. The top guy at a publishing company."

"Oh, come on, you're playing with me."

"No. I just spoke with him, and he's waiting. You need to send him your book immediately." I gave her the paper with Jim's email address.

She looked at it, and said, Is this a joke? This company is a significant player."

"Jim Bennett is at the top. Send it. Don't write a fancy cover message. Just say this is the book Mack talked about, and nothing more."

"But, you haven't even read it."

"It doesn't matter. Jim will. He moves fast and has a million things to do, so you better get it off to him in the next five minutes before he forgets."

"Five minutes?"

"Patricia, go now. If you want a publisher to look at your book, then do it. He'll give honest feedback. Don't worry. He's a good guy and will not rip you off. If he does, then he will have to deal with me. If he rejects the book, then I know other people."

With wide eyes, she scurried off to her room, leaving her cup of tea behind. I sat down and drank it.

She came back ten minutes later, her cheeks red.

"Please have a seat," I said. "Your tea was getting cold, so I drank it."

"That's okay."

I ordered another tea for her and asked, "Did you send your book?"

"Yes, this is insane."

"Why's that?"

"One minute I'm sitting on a hill crying my guts out feeling sorry for myself, and the next, I'm sending my book to a publisher."

"Maybe you had justification to feel sorry for yourself."

"Perhaps, but, I need to seriously think about why I let people spread their distorted values on me.

"What you shared hit home," I said.

"Like how?"

"I have similarities with you, not exactly, but you helped me."

"Really. It's the other way around. You helped me." She paused and peered at me. "May I ask you something?"

"Sure," I said.

"This is not to disparage you, but I'm curious to know how, ah, someone like you would know the top person in a New York publishing company?"

"You mean someone like me who looks like a beat-up caveman?"

She smiled. "You said it, but I suppose it's appropriate."

"It's from a previous life."

"I don't understand, but I'm grateful."

"And, I'm grateful to you."

Patricia's tea came, and she talked, and I listened. She shared about growing up and how she got interested in writing. Her sports were tennis, swimming, and skiing. She liked Asian and Mexican food. She had recently taken up sketching as a diversion from writing. The portrait of me was an example.

As she spoke, something happened. It was as though a weight lifted from her shoulders. She relaxed, and her hands moved freely. Her vocabulary was richer than mine, and I liked how she twisted words and made them humorous. She smiled and laughed, and life came to her beautiful brown eyes.

Patricia uplifted my spirits. She was no longer the somber withdrawn person I had seen during the first three days of the workshop. In the back of my mind, I hoped that a rejection from Jim Bennett would not put her back into a demoralized state.

I had not made any progress on writing a poem about my most important challenge. At least I thought I knew what it was.

* * *

It was a pleasant evening, and the sea gently caressed the shore. Occasionally, the waves jiggled small rocks, causing a swift crunching sound.

I was daydreaming while trying to ignore a heated discussion between Barry and Jade. They were debating the assignment. Then, I heard Barry mention my name.

He said, "I bet Mack here has no challenges. He hasn't said anything about himself during the entire workshop."

"Look who's talking," Jade said.

"What do you mean? I've told everyone about me. We don't know anything about him."

She challenged him. "All you've said is that your feelings are truth. You haven't told us anything about where you are from or what you do, other than you teach in a junior college somewhere in California."

"That has nothing to do with the greatest challenge."

"Rachel didn't ask us to talk about big challenges. We are supposed to think personally. What's your supreme problem? That means you, Barry, whoever you are?"

"When you think about it, the question is meaningless," he stated.

"Everything is meaningless to you. It gets old after a while," Jade said with an angry look.

Barry turned to me. "So, Mack. What's your biggest challenge and did you write one of your juvenile metaphors?"

I saw this as an effort to divert Jade's attack. "I'm still working on it," I said."

Barry laughed. "See. We know nothing of this guy."

Diana and Patricia watched the interchange. Diana said, "I have a different view of Mack. I think . . ."

I cut in. "It's okay. You don't need to defend me. Just let it be."

Barry took a large glug of the rosé wine in his glass. He had been drinking a lot through the meal. Holding his glass in the air, he blurted out, "I've said it all along that Mack doesn't belong in this workshop. It's like a street sweeper attending a Cardiologist convention, totally out of place. It's a waste of time for everyone."

He put his glass down and asked, "What are you anyway, a street sweeper?"

"What if I am?" I asked.

"Well, ah . . . nothing."

"Because everything is relative. Right?"

"Oh, get off it. Some people are just in the wrong place at the wrong time."

"But, during the workshop, you said there is no right and wrong." I was learning to reason like Rachel and Diana.

"Forget it," Barry said. "I see you've ganged up with the girls." He stood up, took the half-full bottle of rosé wine, and walked away.

Jade said, "Whew. For someone who doesn't believe in anything, his behavior says something different."

Patricia smiled. "He's like an electrical impulse without a wire."

Jade and Diana laughed, and Jade said, "He's an airplane without a pilot."

"I've heard that one," Diana said.

"I know it's not original, but it fits," Jade replied.

Diana turned to Patricia and said, "You seemed happy this evening. How are you doing?"

Patricia answered with a grin, "It appears that the school teacher is attentive to the students."

"No, I mean it," Diana stated.

"I realized something about myself today, and it released me. And, I hope to advance my book." Patricia glanced at me, and I gave a slight nod.

"That's great," Jade said. "Let's hope we can all make breakthroughs." She turned to Diana and asked, "Is something different with you?"

Diana smiled. "I made a decision. I've been struggling with a theological question, and while not fully answered, I've found peace. I was fearful of something. As I told some of you, I lost my husband and was struggling about whether to enter a new relationship. My session with Rachel gave a better perspective."

Jade raised her hands. "Hallelujah. So, don't keep us in suspense. What's the conclusion?"

"I made a long-distance call to Africa today. Based on that, on Saturday when the workshop finishes I'll fly from Barcelona and to Amsterdam. On Sunday morning I take an eight-hour flight to Kigali, Rwanda."

"To meet your doctor man?" Jade asked.

"He proposed a few weeks ago when he was in Florida. I kept the poor guy waiting. It took time, but now I sense how God is directing. All the pieces fit, and it seems right. In a few weeks, I will be a married woman with two lovely ready-made kids."

"Well, hallelujah again," Jade proclaimed.

Patricia leaned across to Diana and gave her a hug

Jade saw the waiter and asked, "Could we have a bottle of Champagne?"

The server came over and said, "Here we have Spanish Cava. It is like Champagne."

"That's fine," Jade said. "We need to celebrate."

I ordered fizzy water, knowing the Cava would not be good for my injured head.

As we waited to be served, I asked, "What does your future husband do?" I knew he was a doctor but was unaware of the details.

"He runs a hospital in a rural area in the north-west of Rwanda, where he is also a surgeon. It's not far from the border with Congo. Some churches in the U.S support the hospital, but the needs are great, and most of the time the hospital is missing medicine and supplies. There is a school near the hospital where I will teach."

"Sounds like they need funding," I commented.

Diana smiled. "One needs faith to engage in a work like that."

The waiter served the Cava and fizzy water, and Jade proposed a toast. "May our holy lady of faith find love and happiness."

Diana laughed. "Thank you, but holiness is a free gift for everyone."

"Then, may we all find it," Jade said.

We clinked glasses, and laughter surrounded the table as the women talked about men and love and marriage. Patricia told the story of her book and shared ideas for future books. Jade spoke about running a coffeeshop and how she would make it a success, and how she would start more coffeeshops. Diana talked about Africa. They all babbled on at the same time, and I wasn't sure anyone was listening to the others, but it seemed to be working. I took a back seat.

A full moon rose over the sea, its light shimmering on the water. It was a mystical moment and caused me to think of what or who was behind the universe?

Indeed, Diana was taking a big step of faith. Maybe that was another challenge for me besides the rejection problem. I wasn't sure what I believed.

* * *

The list of ideal qualities of business leaders is long. We are supposed to exhibit self-confidence, determination, and courage to take actions. But, business people crash. We suffer setbacks, strategies go wrong, office politics destroy you, and the most wicked thing of all is burnout. I've known business people who unplugged forever from Wall Street and took shelter in remote rural areas. A room in an apartment is also an option.

My case had more to do with my personal life than with business. I allowed Linette to take away my self-confidence, determination, and courage to act. Business intelligence is one thing. Emotional maturity is another, and I suffered from a broken background. It didn't take much to push me over the edge.

I didn't have faith or a significant belief system to fall back on. When my reference points were gone, there went my identity. An inability to deal with rejection was at the core. Perhaps, by getting this truth on the table, it was the beginning of redemption.

When I got back to my room, I thought about the women in the workshop and our enjoyable evening. They were more relaxed than at the beginning of the week. Diana had decided on a new direction, and she was happy. Patricia seemed like a new person after our discussion earlier in the day and the good news that Jim Bennett would review her book. I hoped she would not be disappointed.

Jade stayed on my mind. She was a bright young woman, and I realized I had misread her at the beginning of the workshop. The initial impression was that she was a bit wild and out of control. Now I saw her as energy-driven. She said she had managed a coffeeshop and tripled the revenue in one year. That's quite an accomplishment. I wish my stock trading results were as successful.

After thinking about Jade's desire to run her own business, I called New York City for a second time that day, this time talking with the real estate agent who had sold me my apartment. I asked him some questions, and he said he would get back to me.

Then, during the night I flip-flopped on my bed. The pain in my head was mostly gone, but the unresolved issues with Linette kept me from going into a sound sleep.

* * *

Friday

The next morning, we were back in the conference room, and Rachel asked if we would like to share our biggest challenge.

Patricia went first and said, "Fundamentally my biggest challenge was confidence. In conforming with the values imposed by contemporary culture, it took away my identity. In the end, I didn't feel I had any worth."

Rachel asked, "So, what made you see things differently?"

Patricia looked at Rachel. "It's funny, but when you and I met, you asked questions that got me to think. And then, yesterday I ran into Mack, and he did something that I desperately needed."

"Which was?" Rachel asked.

"He listened." Patricia smiled and looked at me.

I didn't feel like a hero, because listening was all I could do. Knowing how to respond to her emotions was beyond my capabilities.

Patricia continued. "Then, I gained confidence when Mack helped me, and I learned that a publisher would look at my book." She glanced at me.

"That's wonderful news," Rachel said.

"So, I wrote a little piece to describe my feelings. It's an attempt to look clearly at my biggest challenge."

The greatest challenge,
Is not,

Relationships
or Conformity to a culture.
It is not what they tell you to be.
To adopt the values of reality TV stars,
To wear the latest,
To believe the lies.

The greatest challenge is none of that.
It is identity.

Who am I?
A unique woman with power,
To communicate,
To create,
To love,
To stand confident,
And be me.

Jade and Diana clapped, and Jade cried out with joy, "Now, you're a feminist."

Rachel said, "It sounds more like you're free."

"I'll try to be," Patricia said. "Although, it's terrible poetry."

"Who says so, and who cares? It was written for you," Rachel stated.

"That's right," Patricia confirmed.

"How about you, Diana?" Rachel said, "I understand you made a choice."

"Diana smiled. "A big one."

"Was that your biggest challenge?"

"Not really. It was getting grounded in my faith. I'm a Christian. I had to remind myself of Christ's love."

Barry groaned.

"That's significant," Rachel said. "Did you write anything?"

"I did." She read her poem.

Love is beauty, based in hope,
Found in faith, eternal gift,
Search the universe, search through time
For the savior lifts me free.

"That's cheesy," Barry said. "You can't believe that abracadabra."

"I do," Diana said. "But, I comprehend why you say that. It takes more faith to believe what you believe in than my belief."

"I don't have faith," Barry said.

"I'm afraid you do. Your faith is, it is false to believe in a higher being."

"Well, that's true."

"Then you do have faith. But in going back to our different belief systems, it's uncanny how you continue to use the word 'true'. You have shown nothing to base it on. If faith in a higher being is false, it means we are cosmic accidents, which gives no foundation for truth. Therefore, anything you feel about life, love, and meaning is relative."

"My feelings are the only truth," Barry said.

I felt Diana was wasting time. She was using the same arguments as Rachel, and Barry wasn't listening. His egomania was getting old, but maybe he had a point.

Diana continued, "But, you will never know with finality if your feelings are the only truth. It is a blind leap. How does that stand up when facing the majesty of the universe? Why is it there? Why is there something rather than nothing? And why is there order in just about everything rather than chaos? And, why do humans need to love and communicate? Can you answer that?"

"Sociological evolution," Barry answered.

"But you haven't answered my question," Diana stated. "It seems you have bought into a delusional narrative. Even atheists need answers, and you have given up looking for them."

"God doesn't exist."

"That's quite a statement of faith," Diana countered.

"It's science. We teach it in the humanities, in Social Science and Political Science."

"In today's academia, those fields of study are anything but science."

"My feelings are truth," Barry stated again. "Accept it. Live with it."

"You've said that multiple times, yet that limited worldview has you locked up. That's what makes you such a miserable person." Diana stared at him with piercing eyes.

Barry sulked and didn't reply.

It was like steam in the room, hissing from the mouths of two dragons. When it came to debate, I already decided that I would never mess with Rachel. Diana was now on my list. She was tough. At the same time, I understood where Barry was coming from even though it seemed pretty hopeless to base one's existence only on feelings. Yet, wasn't I like him in some ways?

Rachel intently followed the exchange, and then she smiled and said, "I find this to be a fascinating discussion. If I may redirect this a bit, our goal is to gain an insight into wisdom, which is the ability to discern. One's prism or worldview can temper how we see reality. What Diana and Barry are talking about are two very different perceptions. Of course, the logical question is, which view gives a better orientation to reality?"

Diana spoke out. "If I might give an example, when looking at the world, from my perspective, I can say to God, *wonderful are your works*. That's from Psalm 139. If everything came into existence by chance, then meaning is subjective, including the feeling of wonder."

Rachel nodded her head. "Indeed, these are different ways of looking at reality. Now, let's move on." She looked at me and asked, "Mack, is there anything you discovered?"

I hadn't made much progress. My time had been taken up in talking with Patricia, calling John Bennett in New York, the long meal yesterday evening, and the second phone call to my real estate guy. My fear of rejection was undoubtedly one of my most significant challenges, and I did write something, but it had nothing to do with rejection. Maybe I was avoiding the assignment?

I said, "I thought my biggest challenge was something to do with a relationship. It put me in confines. Now, in taking this workshop, I realize something else needs greater consideration. Therefore, I have written one line." I read from my notebook,

Hidden by opaque layers, my greatest challenge is buried deep. Dig carefully.

"That's it," I said.

"That's lame," Barry blurted out.

It had not been easy to share myself, and his condescending critique made me angry. I growled, "I don't need your commentary."

"It's just helpful feedback," he said. "You need a mentor."

"It would be insanity to consider you as a mentor."

"Screw you," he said.

I stared at him, hoping he'd made a move toward me, for I imagined connecting my lumpy fist into his arrogant face. He smiled and turned in the direction of Rachel.

"Let's calm down," Rachel interjected. "Acuity is a process, and often it takes time to position the critical factors in one's life. Barry, what about you?"

Barry said, "I've thought a lot about this, and there is only one conclusion. My biggest challenge is accepting that people may have difficulty to see my truth because they have a limited view of reality. There is logic in my thinking, and it is as simple as this."

What's true for me is true.
What's true for you may not be true.
If that's accurate, then your voice is a waste of time,
And should not be heard.

My anger continued to boil. I said, "So, the logic is that you silence anyone that doesn't agree with you."

Barry gave a coy grin. "That's a logical conclusion from my basic presupposition."

"So, people should not be free to express an opinion?"

"Anyone is free to speak, as long as they accept my account. Otherwise, let them be silent." He looked me in the eyes and beamed.

I didn't know if he was serious or just attempting to provoke, but he was getting to me.

It seemed like Rachel was tempted to continue the discussion with Barry, but she paused and then turned to Jade, and asked, "Is there anything you discovered?"

Jade looked at her hands folded in front of her. She took a deep breath. "I did a lot of soul-searching and kept coming back to one thing. It's facing a material world without love. In my upbringing, love always came with conditions. It doesn't even feel like love, but instead manipulation. I think that's my biggest challenge. To see this with a new perspective, I have written the following,

Where love is thorns,
Pricks of poison,
Painful deceit.

Flee ruinous talons.

There was silence in the room. I recognized that Jade was talking about her family. At least she had one.

Rachel said, "This shows insight. It's like your greatest challenge is to find a new path. Is my understanding correct?"

"Yes, I made a decision," Jade stated. "I need to break from the control of my family."

"Have you reflected on how to do that?" Rachel asked.

"I'm going to go back to managing the coffeeshop because that brings me joy. And, then I'll explore how to start my own business, with no strings attached from my family. Maybe someday I can have reconciliation with them, but not now."

Jade's poem struck me. I directly related it to my relationship with Linette, for her love had turned into a poisonous thorn. I had to break from the grip of Linette's ruinous talons.

Footprint 7: Think and consider.

A person may think their own ways are right,
but the Lord weighs the heart.
Proverbs 21:2

Go to the ant, you sluggard,
consider its ways and be wise!
Proverbs 6:6

She considers a field and buys it;
out of her earnings she plants a vineyard.
Proverbs 31:16

Rachel said, "Thank you all for sharing your greatest challenges. I know this was difficult for some of you. Doing this is an essential part of the journey to gain an insight into the mystery of wisdom. In going through this exercise, you have put reality on the table, and that's what a wise person does. It wasn't easy, but once the facts were in the open, you attempted to discern them with a new perspective. You have done admirably."

She went to the table next to the whiteboard where there was a small stack of thin books. She took one from the pile, turned to us, and said, "The following exercise for this afternoon is a logical transition. It is to look at how a wise person perceives and acts. There are many sources from what one calls, wisdom literature. These would include such works as Meditations by Marcus Aurelius, Parallel Lives by Plutarch, the Nicomachean Ethics by Aristotle, or Duties by Cicero. These are the works of sages who advise on topics of divinity and virtue."

She raised the small book, and said, "One source that is profound, yet easy to work with is the Book of Proverbs, for it provides contrasts, for instance between the wise and the fool, or the lazy and the industrious. It also abundantly uses metaphors and similes."

She handed out a pocket-sized book to each of us. "The Book of Proverbs has thirty-one chapters, and they are rich with insights and advice. I'd like you to spend some time to identify the characteristics of wise people. For instance, one is that they **think and consider**. That means they contemplate. Things are not taken for granted. They look below the surface. But, there are other characteristics to be discovered."

As a stock trader, I always looked below the surface, although I wasn't so good at doing this when it came to my personal life.

"Look for other qualities of a wise person. Then, using metaphors or similes, try to write a proverb or two of your own. You might apply it to your situation or something different. Be free. We will meet back here in the afternoon at the usual time."

Rachel walked over to Jade and invited her for tea.

I picked up Rachel's booklet and left the room. I walked to town, to the café where I had been before. It was a suitable place to think, and there might be a chance to see Alena.

Then, I thought about the booklet. The workshop was getting weirder all the time, which started with looking at colors, followed by becoming attuned to our senses, exploring our feelings, looking at surrealistic paintings, thinking outside the box and examining our greatest challenge.

Now, we were on a quest to seek wisdom. This workshop was all over the map. I didn't see the logic of where we were headed but knew that Rachel was an intelligent woman and had a purpose in her metaphor-therapy methodology. Still, was it helping to deal with my *constraints*?

* * *

At the café, I took a table under the shade of a tree and ordered a coffee. Barry walked by and didn't notice me, his head focused on the ground in front of his feet. Down the street, he disappeared into a bar.

While waiting for my coffee, I took out Rachel's handout, opened it and began to read. I had never read the Book of Proverbs before.

It consisted of a series of pithy statements that lacked a logical flow, each saying standing on its own. As Rachel had said, it was full of contrasts, such as the wise versus the fool, and the industrious versus the lazy. In one chapter it said, "The way of a fool is right in his own eyes, but a wise man is he who listens to counsel."

That struck me. As far as counsel, I occasionally went to my lawyer, Ben Akerman, for legal advice, but never sought help from others. Was I caught in the prison of my constraints because of that? Was I a fool by doing what was right in my own eyes?

To break out, perhaps I needed to listen more.

I began to speed read through the booklet but then slowed down, seeing that each one was a new continent to consider. To give each saying justice, one had to take time and reflect on it. There were several of the proverbs that advised to think and consider.

The last chapter of the book talked about a wise woman who considered a field and bought it. That was easy to relate to because that's what I did every day when making investment decisions. This woman diversified her assets, that is, she spread her investments out. That's where she had me beat. Most of my money was tied up in stocks, and it would be good to follow her example. Then I thought of the call I had made to the real estate agent in New York.

I came across a proverb that Rachel had quoted in the workshop which said that a fair woman without discretion was like a gold ring in a swine's snout. That was a funny metaphor but drove home the point. Then I thought of Linette.

She had tormented my life. After marriage, it seemed she was never satisfied. She had two main attractions. The first was to spend money, whether on clothing, art, meals in expensive restaurants, or anything else that met her whim.

The second was social events, meaning parties, meeting her friends for lunch, political meetings, or any other happening where she could be the center of attraction. Linette is beautiful, and the eyes of people quickly fall on her, especially men.

In the beginning, it felt good to go places with her. For once I was noticed, of course, because of her. Then, I became jealous when men sought her out. She savored their attention, and sometimes I caught her flirting with them.

Several months after our marriage, Linette became part of a not-for-profit organization that supported environmental causes. Extremely wealthy people backed it. I questioned her motivation because she had never shown an ounce of interest in the well-being of the planet. Her primary interest was herself.

Then, one day I came home from a long day of work and discovered that all her clothing was gone. I tried to call her, but she didn't answer. Then I noticed that she left me a voice message on my phone.

She said, "Hi Mack. I've decided that our marriage isn't working, so am moving in with Preston Healey. I've been seeing him for the past few months and he better fulfills my needs. Today, you will receive the divorce papers. It's unfortunate it ended like this, but it is for the best. Goodbye."

That was a lightning bolt, and for a moment I thought she might be joking. But, seeing the reality of her empty closets drove home the point. Her message was short, expressing little emotion. I played the recording several more times to know if I had heard it correctly. Then, for a long time, I sat in the chair in my office not knowing what to do next. I entered an impasse and then stayed in that state of mind for months.

Preston Heath ran a massive hedge fund, and he was personally worth billions. His photo had been on the front pages of financial magazines, and he was known for taking extraordinary risks in the markets, and they were always successful. He was secretive about his methodology. He was cutthroat.

Her voice message hit me hard, and she didn't return my calls. It was like the universe had imploded.

Shortly after listening to her voice message, the divorce papers came. I put them on a table in the living room without reading them and then suffered through a depressed weekend. The more I thought about it, the more it seemed Linette and Preston were made for each other.

On the following Monday morning, I walked into my office, went to my boss, told him what happened, and resigned from the company.

He tried to talk me out of it, and after realizing he was getting nowhere, he suggested I take some time off. The mutual fund was running well, I had built up a good team, and they could handle it during my absence.

Then, I went to see Ben Akerman, my lawyer, where I gave him the divorce papers. He read through them and said, "Good news."

"What do you mean? I'm devastated."

"She's not asking for anything, no money, none of the expensive paintings in your apartment, nothing. In these papers, she agrees to cancel your prenuptial agreement. She wants a quickie. You can't get a better deal. Sign this, and you are a free man, and you will keep everything."

Our prenuptial agreement was nothing special. It said that we owned everything fifty-fifty. If one person died, then one hundred percent went to the other person. That was it.

I didn't know what to think, for it was like I was living in a hollow chamber with the oxygen sucked out of my lungs.

I looked at Ben and said, "She traded up."

"That's one way to put it. We are talking about Preston Heath. He's the most sought-after bachelor in New York, and she made the kill. She won the lottery, so of course the scraps she left behind mean nothing to her, no offense intended."

"It's okay. I know what you're talking about."

Ben said, "Preston Heath's lawyers probably drew up these divorce papers. My recommendation is that you sign them and get through this as quickly as possible. She's offering you a good deal, and we don't want to get tied up in long legal dealings with those guys. Preston has unlimited legal resources."

I thought about it, and the emotional pain I was feeling was like a barrier that kept me from making the decision. I loved Linette, was obsessed by her, and couldn't bear to see her go. "I can't sign them," I said.

"Then, give it a day or two, and see how it goes," he said.

The day or two had become months. Linette called me numerous times, but I eventually quit talking with her. Then she left voicemails and emails and sent letters. She wanted to marry Preston as quickly as possible. Preston Heath's lawyers contacted me, and they made threats. The more they pushed, the more I went into a state of indecision. Linette was desperate to secure her new-found fortune, and I had no other desire than to lock out the world.

The proverbs about thinking and considering spoke to me. Over the past months, I had not been thinking straight. I hadn't seen reality while suffering from depression and fantasizing that Linette would return to me. The proverb Rachel quoted made sense. Linette was a fair woman without discretion, a gold ring in a swine's snout.

Footprint 8: Speak wisely.

Those who guard their lips preserve their lives, but those who speak rashly will come to ruin.
> Proverbs 13:3

Gold there is, and rubies in abundance, but lips that speak knowledge are a rare jewel.
> Proverbs 20:15

Do not speak to fools, for they will scorn your prudent words.
> Proverbs 23:9

On Friday afternoon I checked my email, and there was a message from the real estate agent in New York. He gave some interesting information.

Then I went to the conference room where the others waited. Barry wasn't there. The last I had seen of him, he had headed into a bar.

Rachel opened by saying, "Previously in the week we explored the use of senses. When rightly used, these become components of wisdom. It's not only to observe details, but also to perceive the dynamics of events and people. It means to understand more deeply."

I understood what she meant. In stock trading, one looked for hidden variables that influenced share prices. I had not considered applying this more broadly, that is, to understand people more in-depth.

She asked, "From the Book of Proverbs, what did you find? Are there other characteristics of a wise person other than the ability to see?"

Patricia commented, "I picked up some things. One of them is that a wise person listens." She glanced at me, and her eyes brightened.

"Where did you get that?" Rachel asked.

"In the first chapter at the beginning where it says a wise person hears and increases in learning."

"There is usually a contrast to each positive characteristic. What would be the opposite of listening?"

Patricia responded, "There was quite a lot about speaking without thinking."

"That's correct. Too many words can get us into trouble. The Book of Proverbs encourages us to **speak wisely**. As I mentioned earlier in this course, the words of the wise are a fountain of life. What else?"

"You mentioned it before, but it is clear that the wise think and consider," Diana said. "The wise do not rush into something without considering it."

Jade laughed and asked, "Like marriage?"

Diana smiled. "Believe me that decision was agonizing and took much consideration and prayer. In Proverbs, many times it says that wisdom originates from God. So, one needs to seek it from him. Yet, do I have doubts? For sure. I am human and one has to be careful about being categorical about everything concerning God."

Rachel said, "That takes us back to something I said earlier. In modern Western thought, wisdom originates from the individual. Older cultures personified wisdom. We see this in Proverbs when it says that she, wisdom, shouts in the streets. Proverbs then goes a step further. Wisdom comes from God where He is the all-knowing being. To be truly wise, one needs to seek him."

"That's my belief," Diana said.

Rachel smiled. "And you may be on a good path, for is it better to put your faith in yourself, or in the omniscient?"

"I have no doubt where to put my faith," Diana answered.

Rachel said, "There is a chapter in my book on wisdom that explores this idea of the personification of wisdom. It is like an integral element in our thoughts and actions."

Diana laughed. "That exactly describes my ideal daily life. It is to engage the ultimate personification of wisdom in everything I do while confessing that I don't do it all the time. It's to engage God in every step."

"The ancient world understood this," Rachel said, "yet we lost it during the Enlightenment, that is, to ask God for wisdom."

Barry wasn't there to groan and challenge Rachel, yet I was sympathetic with him on this one. It was beyond me to think some invisible spirit could know everything, let alone give wisdom.

"Are there any other thoughts," Rachel asked.

I said, "You mentioned it, but a wise person is careful with their words."

"Very good. The wise are gracious and know how to use words for persuasion. Anything else?"

"They are people of action," I said.

"Exactly. Wisdom leads to action. Now after reading from this booklet, did any of you write proverbs of your own?"

"I did," Diana said.

A bumpy path is better than spinning in circles.

Patricia said. "I have one."

Birds of a feather conform together.

Patricia added, "I've done enough of that, and now it is time to be free."
Jade said, "This one is also personal."

A house divided against itself is a materialistic family.

Everyone laughed, for we knew she was referring to her relatives.

They looked at me, and I shook my head and said, "What all of you have written is brilliant. I spent quite some time reading these proverbs, and they triggered much thought. I'm sorry. I couldn't write one of my own."

The saying of the gold ring in the pig's nose was mainly on my mind.

* * *

The session ended, and we had one remaining meeting on Saturday morning. At five I would meet with Rachel and Alena, and then at seven thirty was the group's final meal together. Most of them were leaving after the last session on Saturday, whereas I planned to go on Sunday morning.

As the women left the conference room, I went to Jade and asked, "Do you have a minute?"

She said, "Sure, what's up?"

The room was empty, so we sat down across a table from each other.

I asked, "How serious are you about owning a coffeeshop?"

She waited a moment, and then said, "It's what I want to do, more than anything. I can make a success of it."

"It takes money to start a business. May I ask how you would get it?"

"I've thought about that. It's unlikely a bank would give me a loan."

"What about your family?"

She rolled her eyes. "That's the last thing I'd want to do. My family would refuse because according to them, a coffeeshop is below my dignity. If I did manage to get funding from them, they would make my life miserable."

"Do you have alternatives?"

"The only one at this point is to go back and work for someone else, and then try and save some money."

"Is that what you want to do?"

"Not really."

I waited a moment, hesitating, wondering if I should propose something. The implications meant long-term responsibilities. It implied the end of my hermit existence. Was I ready? Finally, I asked, "May I ask if you've ever considered having a partner in your business, as an investor?"

She paused. "If it was the right person."

"I hope I'm not presumptive, but I was thinking about our previous discussion where you said you'd like to have your own coffeeshop. Out of curiosity, I called a real estate guy in New York who helped me in the past. He sent an email with information about three properties for sale in the city. One in an excellent location just a couple of blocks away from my apartment near tons of financial companies."

"You really did that?" She asked in surprise.

"Did what?"

"Called New York."

"Sure. My idea is this. I propose to pay for the property and become a silent partner. You run the place, and then, we split profits. If for any reason the business doesn't make it, then we sell the property and I take out my initial investment. If property prices drop, then I take the loss. We can define the details when we make a business plan."

Behind this, I was thinking of the woman in the last chapter of Proverbs who invested in property. I needed to start somewhere.

"This is too quick, much too quick," she stated. "Can I think about it?"

"Absolutely."

"I hardly know you," she said.

"Take your time to do due-diligence on my offer and of course, on me. You need to make sure it's the right decision."

"This is unbelievable. Are you joking with me?"

"Does New York City sound like an attractive location for your coffeeshop?" I asked.

"It would be a dream!"

"Then please think about it and let me know your thoughts before you leave here tomorrow?"

"I can do that."

"If you agree to move forward, I'd ask you to come to New York and eventually work out a partnership agreement with my lawyer."

"I'm impressed how you've thought about this."

"Just a bit. I'm better at financial things than poetry." I smiled. "If we do this, you'l have to do most of the heavy-lifting, that is to setup of the place and make it run. I'd be there in the background to help, but you need to be the hands-on manager."

She became quiet, her green eyes round, and she seemed like a deer caught in the headlights. Then, she took a breath and said, "One question."

"What's that?"

"Do you have the funds to buy a restaurant?"

"Enough," I said.

"You surprise me. You're not messing with me, are you?"

"No. It's anything but that." Knowing that someone messed with me and I definitely didn't want to do that to anyone.

"Mack, you're a strange guy. You have been here a week, and we know so little about you."

I smiled. "There's not much to know."

She laughed. "I'm sure there's more to you than that."

"You mean I'm more than a simple caveman."

"You're funny." She paused and took a deep breath. "This is all so sudden. For the past days, I've been introspective trying to figure out myself and my future, and I hit a brick wall. You just created some hope. Thank you."

"You're welcome. Think about it," I said.

Jade left the room, and I wondered if I was doing the right thing. Jade needed help, but I wasn't sure I was meant to be Mother Teresa. It just seemed right. There was more to life than living constrained. One needs to do good in the world.

* * *

At five o'clock, I went to Rachel's house, and she invited me to take a seat on the terrace. Alena arrived shortly after, smiled, said hello, and went into the house.

A few minutes later, Rachel came out carrying a tray with a selection of sliced meats, several kinds of olives, and a small plate with toast and anchovies.

Alena followed. In her right hand, she carried a pitcher with red liquid with chunks of fruit floating in it. In her left hand were three large wine glasses. They sat down and Alena said, "This is Sangria. Do you know it?"

"I've heard of it but never had it. What's in it?"

"It' a base of red wine and Spanish brandy, with a bit of sugar, and slices of oranges and lemons. Some people add other fruits like peaches and apples and even pineapple. We go traditional."

With a long spoon, she fished slices of oranges and lemons from the pitcher and put them into the three glasses.

While I wanted to partake of the Sangria, I said, "Not much for me. I'm getting over a concussion." I tapped the side of my head with my right index finger.

Alena nodded, and she poured half a glass for me and full glasses for herself and Rachel. Her hands glided in elegant, smooth movements, like music.

We clinked glasses, and I sipped the Sangria. It was fresh and fruity.

Then, Rachel spoke. "Mack, we are very grateful for the purchase of the paintings. Thank you."

"I love your stuff."

"Our stuff?" Alena asked.

"Your art."

They both laughed, and I noticed how there was something similar between mother and daughter. They were lovely women. Being with them made me nervous, so I went on to a comfortable topic. "May I ask what it's like to run a hotel and an art gallery? Does it take a lot of work?"

Rachel said, "We have someone who manages the day to day at the hotel, and Alena runs the gallery. This year we have done alright, but if we are honest, your purchase of the paintings helped."

"I'm glad to hear it. Both paintings were a steal."

"If only," Alena said.

"No, I mean it. A year ago, I visited several of the elite art galleries in New York City. It was a buying spree, a moment of folly. Your art is better than what I saw in those galleries, where the prices are sickening."

Rachel said, "It's an odd thing why one form of art is popular, or one artist is a big hit, whereas another isn't. I have my theories, but it is mystifying."

"May I ask how you ended up owning the hotel and gallery?"

"It's a long story," Rachel replied. "The father of my husband was British, and many years ago he moved to Cadaques and bought the hotel and art gallery. My husband eventually inherited the buildings, but we lived in the U.K. Locals managed the hotel, and we spent summers here. My husband died three years ago, so the hotel and art gallery went to Alena and me."

"I'm sorry to hear about your husband."

"It's not easy to lose someone. After he died, we unplugged from the U.K. and moved here, not only to run these businesses, but it somehow feels like we are closer to him."

I felt uncomfortable that the teacher who had such a command of her class was now sharing such personal things.

We drank the sangria and nibbled on the tapas while the conversation went in different directions, about the weather in the U.K. versus the Costa Brava, the satisfaction Rachel felt in running her classes, and Alena's balancing of painting, music and running a gallery. They were glad when October rolled around when most of the tourists were gone.

Eventually, Alena turned to me and asked, "So Mack, how have you endured my mother's workshop. Has it been like walking up a dune?"

I laughed. "You mean, hard work?"

"Yes, and more than that."

"Honestly, it's been a struggle. At first, I wondered what I was doing in there with all those literary types. I was in the wrong fishbowl."

"Nice allegory," Rachel said.

"Honestly, it has been a strange experience, and I still don't have the hang of this metaphor business. But, I see how they force you to see things in new ways."

"That's what poets do," Rachel said, "Although, sadly, some poets are caught up in a game of tinkering with words, rather than bringing a deeper or richer meaning."

"I see that," I said."

"I've come to a belief that in the broadest sense, good poetry enlightens and even leads to truth. The Book of Proverbs is a good example, but there are many other forms of poetry where enlightenment takes place."

"What do you mean by poetry leading to truth?" I asked.

"When Carl Sandburg says, 'I cried over beautiful things knowing no beautiful thing lasts,' you feel there is a sense of truth in this. In his poem, Being Human, C.S. Lewis contrasts angels with humans. He says, that angels, 'see the Form of Air; but mortals breathing it, Drink the whole summer down into the breast.' This is a truthful recognition of the incredible ability of humans to celebrate the glory of nature. These are poems where the reader gains insights into reality and truth."

"That's beyond me," I said.

"I don't think so," Rachel stated. "Something changed in you during the week, like an illumination."

"Okay, maybe. But I have to admit that this workshop got me out of my bubble."

"Which was?" Rachel asked.

I smiled. The psychologist was digging. "I worked in the financial markets and faced burnout, so quit and went on my own. That turned me into a hermit. Therefore, the workshop has been good."

"I'm glad it helped," Rachel said.

"Do you think others have benefited," Alena asked.

"I think so, especially the women." I didn't want to say anything about Barry, because I didn't know where he stood. He wasn't in the afternoon session.

"When do you leave?" Rachel asked.

"Sunday morning, I catch a flight back to New York. I think everyone else is leaving tomorrow."

"What are you doing tomorrow afternoon?" Alena asked.

"Nothing." My priority was getting some sleep.

"Would you like to see Cadaques? It has an interesting history."

I suspected there was little to learn about the village but spending time with Alena was of interest. "That's kind of you. Yes, I would be pleased."

Alena said, "It's the least I can do for one of our favorite patrons. Can you meet me at the gallery at five?"

"I'll be there."

* * *

Later, on Friday evening we had our final dinner with the participants, except for Barry who was nowhere to be seen. Rachel joined us, and the women were in high gear.

At various times during the evening, Jade glanced at me with a pensive look, as though her mind was evaluating alternatives. I had made an offer, and now it was up to her to decide.

After dinner, I went for a walk toward town. It was dark, and the lights from houses across the bay reflected on the still sea. The poetry workshop had been good for me. While I may not have accomplished everything expected in the assignments, I had gained one enormous benefit. It had gotten me out of my apartment.

The thought of my apartment sent waves of apprehension through me. In going back to New York, would I fall back into my old routines?

Linette was my primary concern in going back. She demanded a divorce, which I had been stalling. The week in Cadaques had given me an opportunity to identify a personal weakness. Fear of rejection no longer had to be a disabler.

I now had a better perspective of Linette and our relationship. Her rejection did not need to destroy me, and it was possible to be free from her. The serenity of the evening was like a calming hand, and I made a decision. On Monday, once back in the city, I would see Ben Akerman and sign the papers.

As I came around a bend, I saw Barry walking in my direction. To be more accurate, he was swaying in my direction, and he was talking to himself.

He saw me and with a loud voice said, "There he is. The one who doesn't belong."

"I can't say we missed you," I declared.

He walked up to me and tapped me hard on the shoulder. "You're a nothing," he slurred, alcohol on his breath.

"I thought that was already understood, at least from your way of looking at the world. Everything is nothing. And, because it's nothing, then nothing doesn't exist."

He exhaled a bitter laugh. "Look who got philosophical. I didn't think you had it in you.

Then, he took a swing at me, an unexpected move triggered by drunken irrationality. His movement was slow, and I had time to react, blocking his fist with my left arm. Even so, his hand glanced off the side of my head, and it hurt. I hoped it didn't provoke the concussion or open the stitches.

I grabbed his right wrist and pushed him up against a stone wall. "Stop," I commanded. "Barry, you're going to get hurt."

Instead of fighting back, his body became limp, and whimpered, "This is insane."

"What's that?"

"This entire world, this workshop."

"Why's that?"

"Because I came here for my pleasure and it has been anything but pleasurable. Those women are attacking me. They have no right, Rachel and Diana with their silly argumentation, and Jade not being friendly." His chest heaved up and down, whiffs of sour alcohol exhaling from his breath.

I relaxed my hand from his chest and released my grip on his wrist. "They were just arguing their positions."

"Mack, I'm in a bind and nothing has meaning. There's no hope." His shoulders slumped in resignation.

I wasn't sure what to say. "Barry, I know little about philosophy and meaning, but maybe you've got yourself in a box. I know about that better than anyone because I put myself in a mental prison."

He sneered. "What's your prison?"

"For months I've been a hermit, basically living in a few rooms."

"Oh, come on."

"Believe me."

He had difficulty standing, so I held his arm. He pouted. "No hope. My feelings are a deception."

It seemed he recognized the bleakness of his worldview. Perhaps the poetry workshop had challenged him as it had done with me?

"So, what are you going to do about this?" I asked.

"This what?"

"This no hope, no meaning."

He stumbled a bit. "I'll find answers to the basic philosophical questions."

"What about Diana's answer?"

"I envy her optimism, but that's all it is, belief in a fairy tale."

"Are you sure?"

"Not really, because I'm not sure of anything."

"Then you and I are similar."

"Yeah, yeah," he said. His eyes drooped. "Can you help me find the hotel?"

"Sure, this way."

I held Barry's arm, and we went back to the hotel, and I led him to his room. He plopped onto his bed and immediately fell asleep. I took off his shoes, put them on the floor, and left his room.

Footprint 9: Act wisely.

He was a valiant youth, and his face, like the face of the morning,
Gladdened the earth with its light, and ripened thought into action.
> From, Evangeline: A Tale of Acadie,
> Henry Wadsworth Longfellow

I act for, talk for, live for this world now,
As this world prizes action, life and talk.
> From, Bishop Blougrams Apology,
> Robert Browning

Saturday

I was the first one in the conference room, and Patricia came in with a smile on her face.

She said, "Guess what?"

"I've no idea," I said.

"I received an email from Jim Bennett. He read my book and said he loved it, and he invited me to see him in New York. He asked if I could be there next week."

"That's great news. I told you Jim moves quickly. You'll find him to be a great guy."

"This is just too good to be true, and I only have you to thank."

"I'm glad to do it. Where will you be staying?"

"I hadn't thought of that. Everything is happening so fast."

I said, "I have some unused guest bedrooms. You're welcome to camp out at my place."

"That's too kind. Thank you."

"I'll give you my address and telephone number when the workshop finishes. And, let me say, congratulations."

Jade came into the room, saw me and nodded with her head. We stepped out into the hallway.

She said, "I've given it much thought, and I could hardly sleep. I'd like to explore your proposal, but don't know how to proceed from here. You made an amazing offer."

I smiled. "It's probably helping me more than the other way around. Why don't you come to New York and we can look at available places? We'll do some research to determine which one has the most potential. Then, as I already mentioned, you can see Ben Akerman, my lawyer and work out a partnership agreement. How does that sound?"

"Fabulous."

"When can you get there?" I asked.

"Next week."

"Do you have a place to stay?"

"I have a friend that lives in New Jersey."

"Too far away. Your welcome to stay with me. I have spare bedrooms. Patricia is also coming, so why don't you check with her."

Jade said, "Mack. I don't know what to say. Thank you."

"No. Let me thank you." I suspected it would be a help to have Jade and Patricia around, to avoid again becoming a caveman.

* * *

Barry showed up for the last session. His eyes were bloodshot, and his hair no longer carefully combed across his forehead. He carried a cup of black coffee, took his seat and with a strained voice said, "Good morning." He glanced at me and nodded.

Rachel came in and then summarized what we had done during the week, starting with the first exercise of looking at colors and then ending with an exploration of the Book of Proverbs. In looking back, I found the color exercise to be beneficial, for it forced me into a new way of seeing, of actually observing details. The writing of metaphors and similes didn't come easy, but I understood how they were a way of giving new insights. As Diana once said, "God used metaphors as a way of teaching."

Rachel concluded by saying, "I hope this seminar has been helpful. It was a small insight into the mystery of wisdom."

Rachel said, "In life, it is important to imagine and dream, and make plans. It's also imperative to go outside the box and think like a poet. But, once you've made your discoveries, the most important thing is to act, but make sure you **act wisely**."

In the Book of Proverbs, I had read that wisdom is in the streets and she shouts from the village square. If wisdom were personified, it would be Rachel.

Rachel read a poem by Emily Dickinson titled He Is Alive This Morning.

He is alive, this morning --

He is alive -- and awake --
Birds are resuming for Him --
Blossoms -- dress for His Sake.
Bees -- to their Loaves of Honey
Add an Amber Crumb
Him -- to regale -- Me -- Only --
Motion, and am dumb.

Rachel said, "I challenge you to be alive. Enjoy mornings and blossoms and the bees. Consider creation and the details in the world around you and see in a new way, and through this, be wise. Experience creation and the Creator in fullness. You worked hard this week, and I hope your learning will continue. And, may I congratulate Patricia who found a publisher for her book, and Diana who found a new world."

Diana laughed and said, "You are all invited to the wedding, of course, if you are willing to travel to the middle of Africa."

Except for Barry, everyone in the room was joyful. We stood up and wished each other the best, gave hugs and exchanged emails.

Diana walked over to Barry and shook his hand. They said a few words and then she left the room.

I went to Barry and asked, "Are you okay?"

"Rough night. Rough life," he responded

"Where are you going from here?"

"Back to California. My teaching gig starts in a week, and I need to get my head into it."

"English literature?"

"Yes. This workshop gave me a lot to think about that will help me in my classes."

"If you come to New York, look me up," I said. "I've got guest bedrooms. You'll love the Metropolitan Museum of Art."

He smiled. "With Dali's museum, I was a real ass. I'm sorry."

"We all go through 'ass' moments," I said.

"Thanks for not pounding my face in."

"I seriously thought about it, but realized it had no meaning."

"Very funny."

We shook hands, and he left.

I went to the window and looked out at the Bay of Cadaques. The end of an event can be an emotional time. It was a strange experience to feel a bond with people who six days previously had been complete strangers. I wasn't sure about the outcome of the workshop, but one thing it had done was to break down barriers and form relationships. Now I would be separated from them. It would never be the same again.

It meant I had to go back to the real world and face reality.

* * *

In the reception area, I ran into Diana who had just checked out. She was sharing a taxi with Patricia and Jade. They were going to Figueres, to take the train to Barcelona.

I said, "I wish you a good trip to Africa and much luck with your new life."

"Luck is good, but having God is better." She smiled.

"I wish I had your faith."

"My faith is nothing. What is essential is to believe in the one who is always faithful. That gives a foundation for hope."

"I'll think about that," I said, feeling uneasy with her continual referencing of God. But, I had a question and asked, "You mentioned that your fiancé needs medical supplies for his hospital. Does he take donations?"

"There is a constant need for help. The patients they care for are the poorest of the poor, much more underprivileged than we can imagine."

"How can I give?"

Diana gave me a web address and said, "Are you coming to the wedding? I'm just kidding."

"Am I invited?"

She laughed. "That's a long way from New York, but you are very welcome."

"Then, I'll be there. Send me the date, place and time."

"Are you serious?" She asked.

"Yeah, why not?" I was grateful that she asked and the thought of going to Africa was attractive. I had never been there, and it was another way to break out of my apartment.

Diana hugged me, and I went up to my room. On my laptop, I went to the website she had given me and found the details of where to donate. Then I logged into my bank account and transferred one hundred thousand dollars into the hospital account. It was tax deductible which would make my accountant happy. Many times, he had told me that I should make charitable deductions as a tax-write-off, but that's not the real reason I gave the money.

While doing the bank transfer, I thought about what Diana had said about God being faithful. In New York City, I needed some of that. I needed help.

* * *

At five o'clock I entered the front door of the *Galería de Los Poetas*. Alena was adjusting a painting on the wall, her back toward me. She turned and gave me a great smile. It was genuine, and I couldn't help but contrast that with Linette, whose smile was seductive and manipulative.

"Is that a new painting?" I asked.

"Yes, it is a local artist. I want to help her.

The painting was slightly abstract of a limb of a tree with two birds. I said, "I like the colors, the different shades of yellow, purple and blue."

"She uses an interesting combination, slightly unnatural which gives the painting an edge, yet there is balance in the composition."

Standing back from the painting, I was unsure what she meant, so I switched to the topic of business, and asked, "Do you get many buyers during the winter?"

"Not many. I close during the week, but open on weekends because of an influx of people from Barcelona and France."

I had an idea, and asked, "Have you ever sold your paintings through other galleries?"

"A gallery in London exhibited a small collection. Since moving to Cadaques, I haven't had the time to explore this."

"What would you think if I made contacts for you? I mean for the paintings you do and not for other painters."

"Contacts?"

"Yes. I think your paintings would look good in a gallery in New York. It's a way to expose your art, and the price per painting would be higher than here."

"Do you know of a gallery that would do this?"

"I know several." I had spent a lot of money in some of those galleries. At one, I had spent a bundle on a couple of paintings. The owner's name was Flo Capelle, and she was well connected in the art world. I would start with her.

Alena said, "I never thought of New York."

"If you send me photos of your paintings, that would help. I'll visit some people and will show them the photos as well as the live painting of Poetic Sea, and then we'll see what happens."

"That's a kind offer. Amazing. Yes. I'd be pleased."

"Okay, let's try it," I stated, wondering if this idea would lead to anything.

Alena spent time commenting on a few of the paintings in the gallery and then she asked, "Are you ready for a tour of Cadaques?"

* * *

We left the gallery and walked through the narrow cobblestone streets. On some of the steeper streets, the cobblestones had been vertically placed one next to the other. Alena explained that this allowed the rain to run off more easily. In winter, Cadaques had torrential rainstorms.

Alena described the history of the town. The Greeks and Romans had been here. In the 1500's, a Turkish pirate named Barbarossa, also known as Red Beard, pillaged the village and destroyed the church. The fishermen of the village paid for the rebuilding of the church by fishing on Sundays and religious holidays, and then donated the money.

In the past, the primary economy of the town came from fishing, but now it lived almost entirely on tourism. Artists came here, and of course, Salvador Dali lived here.

"Did you know Dali?" I asked.

"He died before I was born, but my mother and father knew him. Everyone in Cadaques knew him."

"He seems to be an attraction for this village," I commented.

"For that, we are grateful. Dali is like an unseen presence."

We walked through the village. Down one small street, a cat slept in a flower pot, seeming to enjoy the warmth of the afternoon.

The village was small, at least in New York terms. We stopped at the corner of one narrow street, and Alena said, "Salvador Dali is not the only artistic person to come from Cadaques. There were others, for instance, Quima Jaume. They named this street, this *carrer*, after her." She pointed to a plaque on the wall.

"Who was she, I asked.

Alena smiled. "As you can see, she was a *poetissa*, a poet, well known in Spain, who came from Cadaques. An excerpt from her poem 'From Time to Cadeques' goes like this.

Little by little the bay
and filled it with one
magic light, almost divine.
The sea has been condemned
and the boats are like
Somorts after the midnight trance.
A flight of juggling gulls
It evokes in us the love of lovers.

I didn't know what Somorts were, but Alena's soft voice was hypnotizing. "That's beautiful," I said.

"Yes, Quima Jaume had a special sensitivity."

When we arrived at the road by the sea, Alena said, "The oldest part of Cadaques is built on a rocky hill. Look at the buildings pieced together. It's as though they hug themselves to stay alive. The houses are turned inward as a protection, but outwards to feel the sun and sea. You always notice two themes, rocks and flowers, with the stone houses kissing the rocks below them. Then, every little corner becomes a refuge for flowers, mainly geraniums, and of course, the purple bougainvillea's that stretch over walkways. The green shutters on the buildings compete with the blue sea for visual attention, and the honey-colored roofs provide movement and diversity."

I had been in the town for a week but hadn't noticed the details she pointed out, and she described them in such a unique way.

We continued. Alena discretely nodded in the direction of three older men who sat on a bench under a tree. She said, "I often wonder what they are thinking. Because of the mass of tourists that come in the summer, Cadaques has enough wealth to survive, whereas the town has a poor history. Therefore, one questions if our artistry is genuine or commercial, but I think that the dominant presence of that wonderful crazy man tends to keep us honest in our artistic endeavors." She pointed to a statue of Salvador Dali that was near the sea.

"In winter the town sleeps while hiding from the fierce wind, but in spring it awakens to the squawking of the seagulls. Then the tourists arrive, along with transient artists, writers, and musicians. Food and clothing fight for attention, when the coffee bars and restaurants compete with the shops selling hats, dresses, shirts, and jewelry. During that busy time, some of the locals, the real people, hide behind their shutters, waiting for the peace of September when they can emerge and breathe."

Through her poetic descriptions, Alena brought insights I hadn't realized.

We left the village and eventually walked over a hill to the north where we came to a bay.

Alena pointed and said, "That's Salvador Dali's house."

It was a multi-level house built toward the edge of the water.

We found a bench and sat and rested for a while as Alena described her summers in Cadaques, life in the U.K., and her studies. She had gone to one of the best art schools in London and then eventually moved to Spain.

"Do you miss London?" I asked.

"I enjoy the theatre and concerts, although sometimes London seems like an ant colony, with all the movement. Cadaques is a much better environment for an artist."

"I understand, for the 'ants' comparison accurately describes New York City, especially when I look down at the street from my apartment."

"Do you think you could ever move away?" She asked.

"It's funny, but I've been asking myself the same question. Honestly, I could do my work from anywhere. All I need is a laptop and an internet connection."

"Many digital nomads come through our village. What exactly do you do?"

"Ah . . . I look out for investments."

"That sounds like interesting work," she commented.

"There is satisfaction when things go right."

She smiled. "That's how I feel about my gallery."

We walked back over the hill toward the center of Cadaques and then slowly strolled along the road next to the sea.

Alena said, "When I approach this bay, I often think about a poem written by a poet who lived on the opposite side of this body of water. A young Israeli poet name Hannah Senesh was by the sea near Haifa, and she wrote,"

My God, My God,
I pray that these things never end,
The sand and the sea,
The rustle of the waters,
Lightning of the Heavens,
The prayer of Man.

Alena said, "Unfortunately Hannah Senesh was killed during World War II. She had so much potential. She was taken away, and we lost a precious voice."

I noticed the sadness in Alena's eyes. The poem was simple and beautiful, both a poem and a supplication to God. "It looks like this sea has inspired many poets," I said.

"Yes, there are many, like the migratory birds they fill the sky with marvel, and then they leave, but the memory of their magnificence remains."

We wandered back into the village, and I asked, "Would you join me for a bite to eat?"

"That would be nice."

"Can you propose a place?" I asked.

"Yes. How about something simple?"

"That's fine."

On our left the sea was quiet, gently lapping against the beach. Lights reflected on the water, and the boats anchored in the bay were still.

Alena said, "This place can be wonderfully relaxing. Tonight, the sea is soothing and unruffled."

"Just the opposite of New York City."

"The sea is not always like this. It's mood changes, and you should see it when the Tramontana wind blows." Then Alena laughed, and said, "She's like a woman."

I smiled and responded, "I better not say anything, or I may get into trouble, but men can also have their moods."

She said, "When you live here you become aware of subtle differences, you realize that,"

From day to day an endless symphony
Night tunes different from the day
From the depths, she sings her songs,
Not one like another.

"Who wrote that?" I asked.
"I just made it up."
"How do you do that?"
"Grow up with Rachel Eden as your mother." She laughed.
We approached a small restaurant with tables outside, and she said, "Is this okay."
"More than okay," I said.
The restaurant was packed with diners and only one table was free, and a waiter pointed toward it. We sat down, and I ordered rosé wine, and we looked at the menu. I decided to limit myself to one glass, because of the condition of my head.
Alena said, "I recommend Zarzuela."
"What's that?"
"Do you like fish?"
"Yes. I fished as a boy."
"Then, Zarzuela is a surprise."
I ordered the meal, and we sipped the wine and waited. It was a warm evening. Across the limbs of trees around the dining area were small outdoor lights giving a fairytale effect. Old fashioned music played from speakers hung from a couple of wooden beams.
Alena said, "This singer is Edith Piaf, a well-known French singer from the 40's and 50's."
As we waited, I listened to the different languages spoken around us. One table had Germans, and several others had French, mainly older

couples. At others I recognized Spanish, and at two tables it sounded like Catalan. The conversations were animated and filled with laughter.

The Zarzuela came, which was a seasoned mix of fish, mussels, calamari, and potatoes in a tomato sauce, cooked in a large round ceramic dish. The waiter served it onto our plates, and there was plenty left for a second helping.

"You said, Zarzuela was simple. It looks complicated."

"Maybe a little" She grinned.

The meal was delicious, and we continued our conversation effortlessly jumping from topic to topic. Alena explained the differences between French and Spanish cooking and how the food in Spain changed from region to region. We discussed art and poetry, and she filled in for my lack of knowledge of these subjects, while not making me feel like a beginner, which I was. She asked me about stock trading, where I had a stronger footing, and I tried not to bury her in technical details. We laughed about everything from music to politicians, and I felt relaxed for the first time in a long time.

Our conversation opened my eyes. I had been a fool to close myself away from the world while letting fear of rejection control me. There was so much to learn and experience.

We finished the Zarzuela, and Alena suggested small glasses of Garnacha, a sweet wine from the region.

After the wine was served, we took our time. I wanted our conversation to continue. At the beginning of a new song coming over the speakers, two French couples seated nearby got up, went to an open area, and began to dance to the music.

Several people from other tables got into the mood and joined them. It was a delight to see these older couples enjoying themselves, having no inhibitions about being watched, living in and enjoying the moment.

"Do you like to dance?" Alena asked.

"I'm not very good at it," I said.

"It doesn't matter."

She grabbed my hand, and before I knew it, she pulled me over to where the couples were dancing.

"I'm not sure about this," I said.

"Just imagine," she said.

"Imagine?"

She laughed. "Imagine you can do anything."

She placed my left right on the side of her waist and held my left hand with her left. She put her left hand on my shoulder and said, "Now, let's dance."

She pushed my shoulder and moved my hand. The man is supposed to lead, but I wasn't sure what was happening. I was stiff at first and began to relax, and then it seemed we moved in effortless harmony. We danced close, with a gap between our bodies, but at times we touched, and I felt her tall body, strong and feminine, and it sent ripples through me like shimmers in the Bay of Cadaques.

When the song ended, she didn't let me return to the table, and we continued to dance when the next song started, and then, with the beauty of the evening and with the graceful movement of Alena, I lost track of time and space, caught up in an eternal world where only the two of us existed.

After three or four songs, the other couples headed back to their tables. Alena moved close to me, nodded toward the other dancers and said, "It's beautiful to see that love endures." She paused and asked, "Mack, have you ever been in love?"

"Ah, I'm not sure," I said, feeling foolish when I said it, for I thought I had been in love with Linette, but how can there be real love with a relationship based on manipulation? The feelings I had for Linette were more like a desperate dependency. Beyond that, how can someone be in love when they have received so little of it growing up? How can that person even know what love is?

"How about you," I asked. Have you ever been in love?"

She laughed. "Of course, at five years old I had a crush on the postman, and then at ten with a boy who sang in the church choir, and then with a boy-band when I was a young teen, but not yet that eternal love that we see with those couples.

We continued to dance, and mystery filled the evening, like being taken away to a fantasy place.

Eventually, we went back to our table and finished our wine. I paid the bill, and we got up to go.

Alena said, "Thank you, Mack. That was a wonderful time."

I replied, "Thank you for showing me around Cadaques. It made my time here even more special."

Alena looked me in the eyes and with an impulse, leaned in close and kissed my cheek. The delicate softness of her kiss created an electric wave in me more forceful than any found in the ocean.

She stepped back and smiled.

Caught by surprise, I stammered, "That was . . . "

She cut me off and softly said, "Let us never forget this enchanted time."

"Indeed." I regretted that I couldn't find the right words to go with what I was experiencing.

"I must go," she said. "Mack, you are a good man."

She turned and walked away in the direction of her art gallery, and I watched her taking confident strides, like a graceful ballerina.

As she disappeared around a corner, the sweet gentleness of her kiss lingered on my cheek like an entrancing perfume.

* * *

I went back to my room at the hotel, undressed, and went to bed, but couldn't sleep. The workshop had taken me to a foreign place, for it had shaken the foundations of how I saw myself and the world. It had challenged my identity.

Encountering Alena only added to that turbulence. When I first saw the Poetic Sea painting, I became spellbound. Encountering the real Poetic Sea was like finding a mystic realm.

Each moment with her was a discovery. The way she spoke was poetic and beautiful. It opened my eyes and brought life.

I desired more of this. It was like meeting someone who led you from the confines of a dark prison out into the light. When I thought of Alena, I knew a relationship was impossible, because of Linette.

That brought back the reality of returning to New York. I had to see Ben Akerman, for he had the papers and they needed to be signed.

Divorce still seemed impossible. I thought marriage was forever, but what do you do when someone walks away with another person. I believe reconciliation is possible, but how long do you wait for it to happen? The reality was that Linette had deeply hurt me, even ridiculed me in front of my colleagues at the mutual fund. Perhaps that could be overcome, but she made her choice, and I wasn't a part of it.

I fell into an anguished sleep filled with wild nightmares and images far more surreal than any of Salvador Dali's paintings. Emotions streamed through me, of fear and torment and somewhere in the middle of the night I woke up, turned on the light next to my bed, took my notebook and wrote what I was experiencing.

Darkness,
My time is done,
But, where to go?
Go East,
To the water,
Where night fishermen,
Their lights distant flickering stars,
Strung across the sea.

Swim out,
Take a boat and sail forever.

Then a declaration, a voice,
"Imagine,"
It's Poetic Sea.
"Go away," I say, with uncertainty.
She soothes with a gentle challenge,
"Will you know me? Imagine."
She is a multicolored pool,

Majorelle Blue
Lusty-gallant pink
Gingerline yellow.

Consumed by madness,
I crave this abundance,
I crave her dance.

My hands hold a memory,
Her words are sapphires,
Her curves never forgotten,
My tears wash away her soft kiss.

Reality descends,
East it cannot be,
Go west,
Away from Poetic Sea,
To the breaking island of my fear.

I put down my pen and notebook and turned out the light, but the rest of the night was a continual flipping from one side to the other. When a quiet sliver of gray appeared to the east, I pulled myself out of bed, showered, got dressed, and then packed my things into my backpack.

My organized mind had been absent during the week, and I had forgotten to think about transportation to Barcelona. In an information binder on the table in my room, there was one page with a list of taxi companies in Cadaques. There weren't many. I called the first number on the list, and a sleepy voice answered. His English was basic. I'm sure he didn't like to be awakened at such an early hour, but he said he would immediately come to the hotel. I suspected he was glad for the business.

After carrying my bag downstairs, I went to the kitchen where one of the cooks was preparing breakfast. The cook poured coffee in a disposable cup, handed it to me, and gave me a croissant.

I left the key to my room on the desk in the reception area. I had already paid for my stay, so there was no need for a formal checkout.

When I walked outside the hotel, the taxi was waiting. I put my backpack in the trunk, kept my computer bag with me, along with the coffee and croissant, and got into the back seat.

"Can you please take me to the Barcelona airport?" I asked.

He was more than pleased. That was a much bigger fare than a trip to Figueres.

As we pulled away, it was disheartening to leave the *Casa de Los Poetas*.

I slept during the taxi ride to Barcelona and then got lost in the airport with its signs in multiple languages. My instinct was to forget the flight, leave the airport, and go anywhere but New York.

* * *

When I got back to New York City, I took a taxi directly from the airport to the medical clinic near my apartment.

The same doctor who gave me the stitches removed them. He said most of the scar should disappear over time. I looked in the mirror, and it was like spider tracks on either side of a red line. It is surprising that a baseball bat could open the skin like that, or maybe it had been the toe of the attacker's black leather shoes. I still questioned why they did this. Whatever the reason, they had specifically targeted me.

Back at my apartment building, I took the elevator to my apartment and opened the door to darkness. The curtains were closed, and the welcome felt empty and somber, like entering a funeral home.

I went to the curtains and opened them, and light poured into the room, yet it still felt sterile. The colorful paintings and modern furniture should have given life, but I knew what was behind them and they brought me no comfort.

I showered and put on clean clothing. Then, I went to my office and stared at the four impersonal computer screens behind my desk. Somehow, I couldn't turn on my computer. That could wait.

Then, I noticed a few papers on the floor and couldn't remember putting them there. One desk drawer was open, and things on my desk were out of place. I had not left it like that. Someone had been in my office, and there was only one person who could have done this. Linette had a key to the apartment. Why had she come here?

The divorce papers said she didn't want anything. Several times she had told this to me. It was to motivate me to sign quickly.

Adding to the anxiety caused by Linette, my body clock was again messed up by the time change. Europe is six hours ahead of New York. I had adjusted to Spanish time and now had to reorient again.

After the long flight from Barcelona, I was tired, so, lounged around the apartment and eventually microwaved a dinner.

While eating my meal at the kitchen counter, I listened to music on my smartphone, having found "Tchaikovsky's Romance in F minor on the internet. Alena's words came back to me that, Tchaikovsky's works are like sunlight on an iridescent sea. The music made me melancholy, even depressed, knowing I may never see Alena again.

There were things I needed to settle in New York, and I dreaded facing them. To use Rachel's terminology, I needed to put reality on the table. But, was it possible to act on that reality? Linette had a hold on me. Even though she had contemptuously moved on to another man, psychologically she was stuck in my mind like superglue.

I wondered about her and Preston. He was a big-time hedge fund manager. He had made a fortune, but hedge funds involved risks I wasn't willing to take.

Without a doubt, Linette savored her new lifestyle. Married to me, she played with a few million. With Preston, it was billions. The thought of money wasn't the problem. What was painful was that Linette capitalized on my weaknesses and humiliated me. Her rejection had left me in a comatose state.

Playing music on a smartphone doesn't produce the best quality. Tchaikovsky's Romance was sentimental with simple yearning harmonies, and it took me back to the day I stood in Alena's art gallery and heard her playing it on her piano when at times she stopped to repeat certain parts. Then I remembered the evening we danced to French music under the string of soft lights in front of the restaurant in Cadaques. Dancing with Poetic Sea would stay in my memory forever.

Directly after eating my meal, I went to bed at eight o'clock, which was two o'clock in the morning in Spain. The bed felt strangely foreign, for it brought back memories of Linette, and gave the awkward impression that I didn't belong there.

* * *

The following morning, on Monday, while I was eating breakfast, the security guard of the building called. He had a desk in the main lobby of the building. He said that a delivery guy had a package for me, so I asked him to send him up.

A few minutes later, the package arrived. It was large. After the delivery guy left, I opened it, and my heartbeat sped up. It contained the paintings, the larger one of Poetic Sea, and the smaller one with the poem written by Rachel.

I took them into the living room and placed the smaller poem painting on a table, and Poetic Sea on a long sofa. Sitting across from Poetic Sea, I admired the blend of colors, the Majorelle blue sea and the mystery in the sky. Most of all I focused on the movement of the young woman as she floated so gracefully across the sand.

After a long while of musing on the painting, I took a deep breath, stood up, and got my phone. Then I called Ben Akerman, and as it rang, I had doubts. Sometimes, no matter how much you convince yourself of something, deep emotional talons still have a grip on you.

Ben's administrative assistant answered. She said that Ben was busy, but he had a fifteen-minute slot at eleven o'clock. He ran a thriving law firm with a partner, and they had associate lawyers and many support staff. Ben specialized in commercial law but could handle anything.

What I planned to do in his office would only take a few minutes.

I showered and trimmed back my beard. Somehow the beard had become part of me. For the first time in six months, I put on a suit and then went to Ben's office.

Ben greeted me with a firm, confident handshake, and said, "Mack, I hardly recognize you with your new look with the beard and the hair. I like it, but what happened to your face?"

I told the story of getting beat up in the park and about going to a poetry workshop in Spain.

"That's weird," he said.

"The park or Spain?" I asked.

"Both. Anyway, concerning the divorce papers, there's been a development. I don't know if you heard, but Preston Heath got arrested. It's a big deal in the news."

I was surprised. "What for?"

"He took money from his hedge fund and used it for private purposes. Then, his trades turned seriously bad. His investors lost a lot, and the District Attorney issued a warrant, Preston got arrested, and then they took him on a perp walk right into the police station, handcuffs and all. It caused quite a stir."

"Do you think he's guilty?"

"From what I know, they have a stack of evidence, and in spite of his excellent lawyers, he's likely to serve considerable time in prison."

My head was spinning. "So how does that impact the divorce papers."

"For one thing, Linette lost her sugar-daddy. The wording in the divorce papers is clear. She doesn't want anything from you, and she signed them in front of witnesses, and it was notarized. There's no way she can back out."

Ben walked over to his desk and pointed to a large, intimidating stack of papers. He handed me a pen and said, "Now or never. If you don't sign, she is legally entitled to half of everything you have, and she will get one hundred percent if you die."

I took the pen.

He said, "Hold off for just a second." He went to his phone and made a call, and a minute later his administrative assistant came into the room along with another woman, and a young guy in a dark suit, licensed as a notary.

With them watching, I initialed each page and signed my full signature on several pages at the appropriate places, and then wrote the date. Then, I did the same for a second set. The two women signed the documents as witnesses.

When the signatures were completed, Ben handed the documents to the younger man and said, "Officially notarize these." Then, he turned to me and said, "That isn't necessary, but it's better to be covered if your signature is contested."

As the man walked out of the office with the signed papers, it felt like the weight of the universe had left my shoulders.

"Thank you," I said.

"No problem. Let me know if you need further help with this. Is there anything else I can do?"

I thought about Jade, and said, "Yes. I may need help with setting up a partnership agreement."

I explained the potential project.

* * *

Back at the apartment, I changed into jeans, a t-shirt, and tennis shoes. Still tired from the trip, I left the apartment and went to the park and sat on the same bench as nine days before.

The attack by the two men went through my mind. I still didn't have an answer why they knew my name. What was their real intent?

Birds chirped, and sunlight came through the trees. Some leaves on the trees had started to turn color, but it would take a few weeks before they became orange and red.

It was a peaceful place, yet my senses were on alert. Then, I saw a man in dark clothing walking in my direction. He had black leather shoes, and I immediately recognized him. I quickly turned and saw the second man with the bat coming out of the bushes.

A feeling of fear shot through me, but a stronger feeling engulfed me. Anger. My linebacker instincts took over. Without hesitation, I charged directly toward the man in the black shoes. He probably outweighed me, but many times I had met bigger players on the football field.

My attack was unexpected, and the man froze and stood upright, which made a welcome target. After three quick steps I was at full speed, and three steps further I lowered my shoulder and smacked directly into his sternum. He tripped backward, crashing toward the ground with me on top of him, my elbow placed under his chin. His head hit the ground with a deep smacking sound.

Quickly, I rolled off him, got up, turned, and the man with the bat was now rapidly striding toward me. Again, I didn't hesitate but sprinted toward him. That was unexpected, and he tried to stop and pull the bat back into a swing position, but he was slow, and I got to him the moment he started his swing.

As I tackled him, I noticed a detail. In baseball we are taught to hold the bottom of the bat with our opposite hand, that is, a right-handed batter holds the bat with his left hand lowest on the handle and his right hand above his left hand. This man had it the other way around. He was not a baseball player. That explained why he didn't have full power when he struck me with the bat over a week ago.

Like the first man, this one crashed to his back, and with my left hand I took hold of the bat, yanked it away from him, stood up and then swung the bat at full force into his ribs. Unlike him, I knew how to hold a bat properly.

He gave out a deep, rough moan.

I pulled the bat back for another swing, and he said, "No, please." He spoke with an Eastern European accent.

I jabbed the bat into his neck and demanded, "Why are you doing this?"

He held his hands up in front of his face. "I can't tell."

I jammed the bat into his ribs. "Why?"

"Someone hired us."

"To do what?"

"To . . . ah, eliminate you."

"What? You mean to kill me?" I jammed the bat harder.

"Yes."

"Who would do this?"

"A man and a woman. A beautiful woman."

"Dark hair with green eyes?" I asked.

"Yes. That is the one."

I pulled out my phone and turned on the video. Holding it in my left hand, I said, "Repeat it." With my right hand, I kept the bat high above his head.

He grimaced as he stared at the bat, hesitated for a moment, and then said, "A woman with blond hair and green eyes hired us to kill you. We were to use a baseball bat and make it look like the beatings of the homeless people. Only last week we didn't finish it because people were coming. Now, this morning, she called us and said you were home and we should finish it. Otherwise, we don't get paid."

"What was her name?"

"Linda."

"Was it Linette?"

"Yes, that was her name, and the man's name was Healey."

"Heath?" I asked.

"Yes, it was Heath."

I patted his pockets, found his cell phone, and took it out. "Did Linette call you on this phone?"

"Yes."

It was possible to trace Linette's telephone number to this phone, so I put it in my pocket. For the sake of the video recording, I asked, "Is that your partner over there?"

"Yes."

"With the video still running, I quickly walked over to the man in the black shoes who was knocked out cold and filmed his face, his clothing, and his shoes. I turned off the video, and then went back to the conscious man. He had raised up to his hands and knees.

I said, "This video is going to the police, and I'm sure they have both of you in a database, and they will come looking for you. What you do between now and then is up to you, but I recommend that you leave the United States and never come back again. Attempted murder is a serious offense."

I left the two men and headed toward my apartment wondering how Linette knew I was back in New York?

* * *

The walk gave me time to think. Linette told those two thugs to get the job done. Having been gone for a week, how did she know I was back home? Without having many ideas, I suspected she had bugged my apartment. Whatever happened, I needed to be wise.

Back in the apartment, I looked around. In the living room, nothing seemed unusual or out of place. Knowing there were papers out of place in my office, I went there, sat in my chair, while attempting to behave like everything was normal.

At a bookshelf along one wall, I noticed a book that hadn't been there before. It had a small dot on the spine. I was sure it was a camera.

I went into my bedroom, looked around, and didn't see a camera, so opened a closet. In it, I had a few paper supplies. After finding a letter size manila folder, I wrote my name and address on it. Then I took a few printed pages out of a binder, stapled them together and put them in the manila folder. Then, I went back into my office, sat down, and made like I dialed a number on my cell phone.

I figured the camera setup included a microphone, so I said, "Ben, do you think I should sign these divorce papers?" I raised the envelope in the air so that the camera would see it.

I waited for a second, then said, "To be honest, I'm not sure about signing them. I need to talk with Linette. I'll give her a call." I pushed a button on my phone, as though I hung up.

Then, I called Linette's number.

She answered on the first ring.

I said, "This is Mack. I was out of town for a week and just got back. I'm still not sure about signing the papers you sent to me. I had them here and wanted to give you good news, at least for you. I'm ready to sign them." Again, I lifted the envelope in the air.

"Mack, wait a minute. I have second thoughts. Can we talk?"

"About what?"

"I have ideas and hope you would hear me out."

"Okay, but can you come quick?"

"Yes, I'll be at our apartment in twenty minutes."

I liked the way she said, 'our' apartment. Months ago, she abandoned the place. "I'll wait," I said.

I hung up and immediately took the envelope into the living room. After getting my laptop from its bag, I opened it, set it on a table and opened the video record function.

I went to a closet and got an older laptop, put it in another area in the living room and opened video record.

After getting an old smartphone from the closet in my bedroom, I put it on a shelf in the living room and set up the video record function. I kept my regular telephone in my pocket, for it had the video of the two thugs in the park.

Then, I called the security guard and asked him to call me when Linette arrived.

I waited while working out a plan. It was difficult to think straight, because of the mountain of anger I was feeling. In thinking of what I had learned at the workshop in Cadaques, I controlled myself. I would observe, listen, consider and act as wisely as possible. Fundamentally I was dealing with a snake.

After fifteen minutes, the security guy called, so I quickly went to the laptops and telephones and turned on the record features.

My heart beat fast. I didn't know what it would be like to see Linette. She had deeply hurt me and sent me to purgatory.

The bell to the front door sounded, and I went to it and opened it, and a moment later Linette rushed into my arms. It seemed she had been crying.

"What's wrong?" I asked while faking compassion, while gently moving her away from me.

With a shaky voice, she said, "I made a huge mistake, and I ask you to forgive me."

"For what?"

"It was foolish for me to see Preston. He manipulated me when I was at a weak moment. You know it was short lived and I never really moved in with him."

Part of that was technically accurate. He had set her up in a guest apartment attached to his gigantic mansion, but she stayed in the house with him.

"So, what do you propose," I asked, motioning for her to come into the living room.

She saw the painting of Poetic Sea and asked, "What's that?"

"It's a painting."

"Who is the painter?"

"Someone you wouldn't know."

"Oh, Mack. You should never buy a painting from an unknown. It's too risky. See, you do need me to help you with these things."

"I like the painting."

She peered at it for a while and said, "Yes, it does have compelling features, but even so, you should put it in a bedroom."

"But, I like it."

"Yes, but. Okay, it does have potential, and you may have made a fantastic choice."

I understood that she was attempting to gain control, and I needed to go carefully. For a long time, I had been under her malicious spell. As Linette talked, I was struck by her beauty, with an innocent face and a perfect body. Her green eyes were seductive tools. She wore designer clothing and high heel shoes that brought out her long slender legs. For many men, she was a dream.

I asked, "What do you think about the divorce papers?"

"I would implore you not to sign them. It would be a mistake. I love you and know you love me in your deepest heart. You are a forgiving man, and we can live the most wonderful life imaginable."

"Until the next billionaire comes along," I stated.

"What?"

"You heard me." I gave her an icy stare. "Did you notice my face?"

"Yes. What happened?"

"It was much worse a week ago. It wasn't pretty. Some men attacked me in the park and tried to kill me."

"Oh, you imagine things."

"It's reality. It was two thugs from Eastern Europe, and someone hired them to do it."

"What are you talking about?"

"It was you Linette with the help of Preston."

She gave me a condescending smile. "You're hallucinating."

"Watch and listen to this." I played the tape of the man and his confession. When he mentioned Linette's name, her face hardened.

"He's lying," she said.

"Not really. There's something else. In my office, someone installed a surveillance a camera. I bet your fingerprints are on it."

"Stop it, Mack. You are angry. You don't know what you are saying."

"Preston Heath has financial and legal problems, so the two of you needed a source of funds. With him locked up, you lost your unlimited bank account, so the contingency plan was to remove me. Then you would get one hundred percent of my fortune. It would pay Preston's legal fees, but I bet you have no intention to give him any of it. Although, there was one hitch along the way."

"What's that?"

"In the divorce papers, you gave up your rights to my wealth. If I signed the papers, you would get nothing. That's why you searched my office. Your fingerprints are all over the drawers and papers that are out of place." I was only guessing when I said this.

Her lower jaw jutted out, and I imagined venom dripping from her tightly clenched teeth.

She blurted out, "You are a horrible person. Yes, Preston and I hired them and paid them, but those idiots failed on the first try, and today I instructed them to finish the job. Did you sign the papers?"

"Yes. It's a done deal."

"But, they are in the envelope. Earlier you were talking with your lawyer."

I smiled. "I see you've been paying attention to your spy camera."

"You can destroy the envelope and what's in it," she declared.

"Sure, if you want." I handed the envelope to her.

She opened it, saw that the contents were not the divorce papers and her face became red. She hissed, "I will fight it in court."

"Good luck."

"I know how to manipulate people," she claimed. "A jury will be putty in my hands."

"I have no doubt that's true, but now, I have evidence."

"What evidence?"

"The confession of those two men."

"That's nothing."

"And, the confession you made a minute ago."

"What do you mean?"

"You are not the only one with a camera and a recorder." I circled my finger around the room.

She froze, then looked at me as though she had nothing more to say.

I said, "I've been thinking, and somehow this evokes a feeling for you. You need to listen to this." I had printed out a poem by, Robert Frost and read it to her.

Some say the world will end in fire,
Some say in ice.
From what I've tasted of desire
I hold with those who favor fire.
But if it had to perish twice,
I think I know enough of hate
To say that for destruction ice
Is also great
And would suffice.

Linette sneered and asked, "What's this? Have you gone crazy?"

"Maybe, but that poem communicates something. Life with you has been miserable, fire and ice. You burned me, and then my emotions froze to numbness. Now, having come to my senses, I wouldn't wish you on anyone. Those recordings are going to the police, and I'll let them deal with it. Attempted murder is serious. The police will receive the recordings within one hour. Of course, it will take them a bit of time to analyze this. Then they need to produce a warrant. Then, they will come looking for you. When the police learn you are a partner of Preston, an accused felon, that will make it even worse. They will tie you into his defunct financial affairs and illegal dealings."

Her face became ashen, eyes wide. "I had nothing to do with Preston's business dealings."

I said, "Soon, they will be after you. What you do between now and then is up to you, but it won't be healthy for you to stay in the State of New York, or even in the country. Now, please leave."

I stood up, and she slowly did the same. She walked to the front door as though lost in the fog. She began to cry, and I suspected that her tears were genuine. But, with Linette, one could never be sure.

* * *

I faced choices. One was to give the evidence to the police and see Linette get arrested. In that case, I'd be forced to live through months of legal proceedings. She was right about one thing. Without a doubt, she could manipulate a jury. I imagined gossip magazines at supermarket checkout stands with headlines like *Beaten Wife Hires Thugs to Kill Millionaire Husband.* Did I want to live through months of endless court proceedings and journalists knocking on my door?

The other alternative was just to let it go. The divorce was in progress and needed finalization. If Linette or those two thugs reappeared, I had the recordings. I planned to give a copy to Ben Ackerman and keep another copy in my safety deposit box at a bank.

My only concern was the future damage that Linette could do to someone else, and I carried a bit of guilt about that.

Three days after I got back from Spain, Patricia showed up. I had almost forgotten about her. She asked if I would like to go with her to see Jim Bennett, but I declined, sensing it would help her confidence to go on her own.

After seeing Jim Bennett, she was elated. Jim's company would publish her book. There were contracts to be signed. Patricia was offered a sizeable advance, which is rare for a first-time author.

Jim called and thanked me for sending Patricia to him. He was confident her book would be on the best seller list. He also sent a print-out of his portfolio for me to analyze, which I was happy to do. I'd do anything to keep from going back into a hermit existence.

Jade showed up at the end of the week, and the following week we visited properties, talked with a market research company, and worked out financial scenarios. Eventually, we decided to purchase the small restaurant just a couple of blocks from my apartment. Thousands of people went by that location each day, and every business person on their way to work is looking for a gourmet cup of coffee and something to eat at lunchtime.

Jade planned to serve simple but healthy food, as most people in that area are not looking for long sit-down meals. She met with Ben to draw up our partnership agreement.

She decided to call her coffeeshop, *Jade's Place.*

During that second week, I received a set of photos of paintings from Alena Eden, so I called Flo Capelle and invited her to come over to my place to see the photos, but mainly to see the painting of Poetic Sea. Flo knew everyone in the art world and could evaluate if Alena's works had potential.

Flo came over and spent a very long time looking at the Poetic Sea painting. Finally, she said, "I'm impressed. This painting is unique."

"How much do you think that would sell for?" I asked.

"A lot." She quoted a price four times what I paid for it.

"And, what about the ones in the photos."

"I'd have to see the actual paintings, but they could do quite well, especially if we can develop the artist's name."

"She could use some help. All I can say is that I took one look at that painting and it did something to me." I pointed at Poetic Sea.

"It lifts you to another place," Flo commented.

"And, what about the second painting, the one with the poem? Could you sell paintings with poems?"

She concentrated on it for a moment and said, "It's a fascinating concept. We can give it a try."

I gave her Alena's contact details. After Flo left, I got busy with other things.

During my running around, Barry sent an email. It was nice. He said he was preparing courses, and that, "This time I'll focus on students rather than myself." He apologized for things he said in Cadaques and explained he was going through a particularly dark period while trying to find his way. I knew what he was describing. He also said, "I'm evaluating philosophical alternatives," and, that he had contacted Diana. They were having a "dialogue." I replied and did my best to send words of encouragement.

After two weeks back in New York, I pulled out my notebook from Rachel's workshop. It triggered memories. Some of my metaphors were atrocious, and I laughed.

Brown like a brown pine needle.
Blue sea like deep blue water.

Another one wasn't exactly a metaphor, but it indeed expressed my feelings.

Empty and not even wanting a refill.

The other participants in the workshop were literary. I was not, but I did gain a small insight into the mystery of wisdom, as well as a big realization about myself. Rachel was perhaps the most intelligent and wisest woman I had ever met. At the same time, Cadaques now seemed remote.

Each day I looked at my Poetic Sea painting, and I felt a pang of emptiness. It reminded me of dancing with the real Poetic Sea. It reminded me of the unfinished portrait of the young Alena Eden, with the sea in the background, and the girl's eyes staring into your soul. Then I connected my emotions to the agonizing poem written during my last night in Cadaques,

Consumed by madness,
I crave this abundance,
I crave her dance.

With all that happened since returning to New York, that weeklong event in Cadaques seemed unreal. I guess that's how it is in life. We move on to new things. Each experience gets replaced by another.

* * *

During the third week after returning from Spain, things became hectic. Jade moved extremely fast. She began the interior design of her coffeeshop, bought equipment, and interviewed potential employees. I tried to stay out of it, but she often came to me for advice.

Patricia started to write a new novel, and my office became her writing center. I didn't mind, preferring to work in my bedroom.

Finalizing the divorce took up much of my time. We had already completed a ton of paperwork, but there was more to do. Ben Akerman and I went to court, and Linette's lawyer was there without her. Her lawyer had power of attorney, so her presence wasn't required. He turned out to be cordial and helpful. It was clear from the paperwork that the divorce was uncontested, and it seemed her lawyer wanted to move on to other cases. He was probably already paid for his work, and with Preston Heath in jail, there wouldn't be money available for lengthy litigation. And, I guessed he didn't want to take on Ben.

The judge gave a signed Judgment of Divorce, and Ben filed it in the County Clerk's office. Divorce is messy and bureaucratic. Linette was nonexistent through the entire process. When finally finished, it was a relief, but I felt shell-shocked and needed to get away.

I wasn't ready to face hectic New York City, so booked air tickets and flew to Rwanda, asking Jade and Patricia to look out for the apartment. They were two lovely women, and under normal circumstances, I'd be attracted to them, but with frazzled nerves, I needed space from relationships.

Once I got to Rwanda, I stayed three days in a nice hotel in Kigali, the capital. It gave me time to get over jetlag and to acclimate to Africa. During those days I walked along the streets which were teeming with activity. I found the Rwanda people to be polite. They didn't make much eye contact, but occasionally, it was evident that a large white guy with long hair and a scruffy beard gained their attention.

Then I hired a driver, and we headed north-west on a four-hour trip to the town of Gisenyi, which is on the north of Lake Kivu. I had never heard of Lake Kivu before, but it is one of the largest lakes in the world. The lake forms a border between Rwanda and the Democratic Republic of Congo to the west.

Diana was happy to see me and introduced me to Peter, her fiancé, and his two children. The kids were thrilled to have her as their new mother.

She told me that Barry had contacted her, and they were communicating. He was asking honest questions about her 'philosophical construct,' as he put it. Diana called it something different. Faith in a loving God.

Peter's hospital was as Diana had described it, basic, but functional. It lacked medicine, and they did their best to treat people from the area, including those coming across the border from Congo. They gave medical care to the poorest of the poor. Peter said he was speechless when they received my donation. After seeing their needs, I decided to send more funds.

The wedding took place in a church in Gisenyi, and Diana was radiant and beautiful. The African singing was fabulous. I don't know if it was the jetlag or the change of environment, or the aftermath of what I had gone through in New York, but when they sang a song titled *Oh the Deep Deep Love of Jesus*, emotions overwhelmed me, and tears came to my eyes. I discretely wiped the tears hoping no one would see.

The pastor gave a talk on love, particularly Christ's unconditional love. He also talked about the sanctity of marriage, and for a moment I felt guilty. Getting over the painful experience with Linette would take time.

As the pastor spoke, I glanced at the words on the song sheet.

O the deep, deep love of Jesus, vast, unmeasured, boundless, free!

Rolling as a mighty ocean in its fullness over me!
Underneath me, all around me, is the current of Thy love,
Leading onward, leading homeward to Thy glorious rest above!

The words hit something profound in me, and for the first time, I said a simple prayer.

God, I have not had much real love. Thank you for your love.

When I said that, a sense of peace filled me, and I wasn't sure if it was from the beautiful voices of the Rwandan singers, the words of the pastor, the fact that I was now free from Linette, or the insights I had gained from Rachel Eden. Or, did that peace originate from the message of love that Diana had shared? She said God's love is eternal, which means there is no rejection. Whatever it was, there was an impression that something changed within me.

The wedding reception was at a restaurant along the lake, with a large lawn. The food was simple but delicious. I took a lot of photos to send to Patricia, Jade, Barry, and Rachel.

During the reception, I had a quick discussion with Diana and Peter. I didn't want to interfere with their honeymoon plans and all that business, but I gave them a wedding gift, plane tickets to fly with their two kids to the island of Zanzibar, plus a two-week stay at a resort hotel. I had bought the air tickets and hotel package at a travel agency in Kigali. I knew little about Zanzibar, other than it sounded exotic, and the photos on the tourist brochure were fabulous.

Diana and Peter were very grateful for the gift and Diana led me off to the side of the reception area. She said, "During the workshop in Cadaques I sensed you were unsettled. I've prayed for you, hoping you can find peace."

"Thank you," I said. "Something happened during your wedding ceremony. I realized something about God's love."

Diana smiled. "I'm happy for you. It will make all the difference. I will pray that He gives you wisdom."

"I need that," I said, thinking of the 'footprints' outlined in Rachel's book. "I have felt lost over the past months, and need direction."

She said, "There is a verse that says, *My goal is that you may be encouraged in heart and united in love, so that you may have the full riches of complete understanding, in order that you may know the mystery of God, namely, Christ in whom are hidden all the treasures of wisdom and knowledge.* He is the One who can give you direction to something good."

"I understand," I replied.

Diana hugged me and then went back to be with Peter and the rest of the guests at the reception. In watching the newly married couple, I had the impression there was something symbolic in marriage, more than just a contract between two people. I stood off by myself reflecting on the verse that Diana had quoted. I needed to find it in the Bible for it matched what Rachel had said about the personification of wisdom, that it originates from God. It was only a matter of asking and trusting, and He would give it.

After a week in Rwanda, I considered going back to New York, knowing that at some point I needed to start doing some stock trading. But, my heart was still not in it. It would come.

Instead, I set my sites on Europe. My return air ticket went from Kigali to Amsterdam to New York, so I decided to stop off in Amsterdam. With first-class tickets, one has a lot of flexibility in changing itineraries. Five weeks ago, I would never have dreamed of this. For the months before that, my most far-reaching expedition had been to a park bench.

* * *

Amsterdam was a contrast to Kigali, with its canals and narrow brick buildings. Many people were blond with blue eyes, and they spoke loudly. Their laughter was infectious, and one felt freedom in the air. It was

October and the weather in the morning and evening was chilly, with a fresh wind blowing off the North Sea. People are taller than average in the Netherlands, so I had no problem in finding a jacket my size.

I took a boat ride on the canals, saw the Van Gogh Museum, and the Rijksmuseum where there are numerous Rembrandt paintings. Restaurants were numerous, having every type of food under the sun. I needed a few days on my own but then feared that I might drift back into hermit mode.

After three days in Amsterdam, I looked at a map and decided to head to Paris. I traveled with just a backpack and computer bag.

For another three days I did the same thing as in Amsterdam, wandering around Paris, taking a boat ride on the Seine River, visiting the Louvres, Orsay and Rodin art museums, and eating fantastic meals. On the fourth day I walked to the Paris Gare de Lyon train station and took a high-speed train toward the south-east, to the city of Lyon, thinking to connect to a train to Switzerland the following day.

I arrived in Lyon in the early afternoon, found a hotel and took a long walk next to the Rhone River. In the evening I ate in a fabulous restaurant that seemed straight out of the 1930's, with high ceilings and giant chandeliers. The waiters wore long-sleeved white shirts with black ties and black aprons. There was none of the introduction business that you find in the U.S., like, "Hello, my name is Sam, and I am your server this evening." Nor, did they come back to you every three minutes asking, "Is everything okay?"

These waiters were all business, taking orders and carrying large round trays loaded with plates of food. They moved with speed and efficiency. I ordered *Poulet de Bresse à la crème et aux morilles*, which the waiter explained was typical of that region in France. He recommended Condrieu white wine. My knowledge of wine was limited to California Chardonnay. I ordered one glass.

Indeed, the chicken was delicious, cooked in a cream sauce with mushrooms unknown to me. The wine was dry and slightly fruity and went perfectly with the chicken.

The restaurant was full of animated people enjoying their meals. I was the only one eating alone. That gave me a strange feeling and raised a question. Was I to spend my life on my own? Sure, the meal was fabulous, but wouldn't it be better to share it with someone?

My thoughts went to Cadaques and Poetic Sea and the Zarzuela I had with her. Wasn't that the best evening of my life? It made me realize that it isn't the quality of the food that's important or the price on the menu. What matters the most is who you are with.

Then I became troubled. I had just gone through a terrible time in life, and the divorce was anything but fun, an emotional and administrative nightmare to live through. It was too soon to be thinking of anyone else. With a guy like me, maybe I should never think of having another relationship.

My idea was to travel from Lyon to Switzerland. I always wanted to see that country with its snow-covered mountains, chalets in quaint villages, and cows with bells. The image of Switzerland somehow reflected tranquility.

I finished my meal and went back to my hotel, with a plan to head to Switzerland in the morning.

Footprint 10: Ask God for wisdom.

Great is our Lord and mighty in power;
his understanding has no limit.
Psalm 147:5

If any of you lacks wisdom, let him ask God, who gives generously
to all without reproach, and it will be given.
James 1:5

That night, I dreamed a lot. *Poulet de Bresse* is delicious, but probably best not to eat in the evening. I tossed and turned, and the meal wasn't the only cause. Cadaques kept going through my brain.

It was a relief when the light of morning came. I got up, showered, dressed, had breakfast, and then walked to the Lyon Part Dieu train station.

While waiting in the line to buy a ticket, I looked at a large electronic board showing train departures. In fifteen minutes, there was a 'TGV' fast train leaving south for Barcelona, Spain. The train going east to Geneva, Switzerland left in two hours.

A decision was needed, one having more implications than any stock trade. Then, the words of Rachel came back to me. Wisdom originates from a divine being outside themselves.

Diana was more specific by stating that wisdom is found in Jesus Christ. She had said, **"Ask God for wisdom.".** Without engaging Him, it's like making decisions by viewing through an opaque window.

Looking up at the departures-board, in desperation I whispered, "God. What shall I do?"

A lightning bolt didn't fall from the sky, but I knew where my heart was tugging.

When my turn came to buy a ticket, I asked the ticketing agent, "Does the Barcelona train stop in Figures?"

He looked at me with an expressionless face and said, *"Oui. Voulez vous un billet?"*

I guessed that to mean, do you want a ticket? I said, "A one-way, first-class ticket to Figueres, please."

He gave a small, almost imperceptible nod, and printed out the ticket.

I made the payment, took my ticket, and got on the TGV to Figueres. I heard some passengers speaking English, and one said that the TGV regularly reached speeds of two hundred miles per hour. Indeed, the train seemed fast as it zipped through the French countryside. Through much of the journey I slept, because of my unsettled night.

When the train reached Figueres, I got off and took a taxi to Cadaques. Five hours after leaving Lyon I stood in front of the *Casa de Los Poetas*.

As the taxi drove away, I stared at the front door of the hotel and after some hesitation, made my move. There was no reason to turn back now.

I went into the lobby and found the same woman as before behind the reception desk. She saw me and hesitated a moment as though she tried to place me. Then, she smiled and said, *"Buenos tardes senior Mack."*

"You remembered me," I stated.

"Si, si. You are someone easy to remember."

"Would you have a room for one night?"

"Of course. It is now October. In August we are full, and without reservation you would sleep on the beach."

I laughed and said, "Thank you."

She gave me the same room as my previous stay, so I went into the room, left my bag and went back to the reception desk. "May I ask if Rachel is around."

"Yes, she is at her house."

"Would it be possible to see her?"

"Now?"

"Yes, now."

The receptionist called a number and spoke Spanish. I heard my name spoken and understood a few words and phrases.

She hung up and said, "She is happy to see you. Go to the terrace of her house."

I left the hotel and walked down the path to Rachel's house. She was waiting on the terrace, and she smiled and waved when she saw me. She looked beautiful, as always.

I approached her and held out my hand, but she bypassed it and hugged me.

"Mack, it is so good to see you. Indeed, this is a surprise."

"I was in the area, so wanted to stop by," I said with a sheepish grin.

"I don't believe you one bit, but please sit down. You look different."

"The bruises are gone, and the hair is a bit trimmed."

"You look civilized, or just enough." She smiled. "The scar is still there but healing."

"Now, I can almost look at myself in the mirror," I chuckled.

She smiled. "Can I get you something to drink?"

"Water would be fine."

She left, I sat down on one of the chairs and looked out toward the sea. It had been over a month since last sitting there when I met with Rachel. She had questioned me, and I was not forthcoming, fearful that 'a shrink' would dig into my brain and discover hidden secrets about my closed-off existence. Now, I felt more confident, and my situation was different.

Still, I had a question, and I thought that Rachel might give me insight.

Rachel came back with two glasses of water, then said, "Please tell me what you have been doing? Alena told me about the art gallery in New York and how you made the introduction, not only for her art but also for my poem-art."

"Flo Capelle, the gallery owner, loved Alena's paintings, and yours, but I've been swamped and haven't had time to follow up."

"What have you been up to?"

In the past, I was reluctant to share myself with Rachel. She knew little about me. But, I told her everything starting with my mutual fund, Linette, and my life as a hermit. I told her about being attacked the first and second times, my encounter with Linette, and the divorce proceedings.

Occasionally, she asked questions, but mostly she listened.

I told her about Patricia and Jade, and about the emails with Barry, and I described Diana's wedding.

She was pleased to hear the news and surprised I was communicating with Barry.

I said, "It turned out he was going through a difficult time. The workshop was tough on him, and Diana and Jade didn't back down when he challenged them. But, he said that's what he needed. You didn't either. It shook him from his introspective narcissism, as he called it. Of course, I just wanted to smash his face into the dirt."

"I admired you for your patience," she said.

"Patience? It was more like I was numb to the world. The workshop not only helped Barry. It also helped me."

Rachel said, "I didn't tell anyone, but Diana and I quickly realized something about Barry. For the first two or three days of the workshop, he plagiarized all his metaphors and poems, picking straight from well-known poets and writers. Diana and I challenged him on this. I didn't feel it was helpful to validate his actions."

"It seems something changed. In one of Barry's emails to me, he wrote that he enjoys teaching again. He has also been communicating with Diana about, philosophical stuff, as he calls it."

She laughed. "That's good. People can become bound by conjectures, and it's sometimes beneficial to question them."

"You mean, like a prism that distorts what is real."

"Exactly. You are a good student."

I wanted to ask her a question but hesitated. She spotted this and said, "That's quite a story you told me, and I certainly didn't know that about you. I'm sure the past year has been tough on every level, but it looks like you are on a positive track. Is there anything else going on?"

I didn't know how to get into it, so said, "Do you remember the paintings I bought from your gallery?"

"Absolutely. You made good choices." Rachel grinned.

"Both are now hanging in my apartment in New York, with a Jackson Pollock in the middle."

"Pollock? Wow, we are in good company."

"I could get rid of the Pollock and not miss it, but the other two are meaningful to me. I look at them every day but am especially drawn to the girl walking by the sea."

"I know her." Rachel smiled.

"I wanted your advice, and maybe my questions are not logical or in the right order, but do you think it is too soon to visit the girl by the sea?

Am I ready? And, do you sense she would accept that? I would like your honest thoughts."

Rachel looked at the sea for a moment, like she did in the classroom and I knew she was thinking. She said, "Mack, I am a psychologist, but you and I must never have a doctor-client relationship. We must always be friends."

"I understand that."

"As far as time, it seems it was over seven months ago that Linette left you. Before that, it appears that you had a dependency on her. It wasn't co-dependency, because she seems to have egocentric tendencies. That's now behind you, and it looks like you've found self-assurance and orientation. If you are ready, I encourage you to explore relationships, but try and find the right one."

That gave me confidence, but my question wasn't answered. I asked, "Would it be okay if I visited Alena, and do you think she would consider someone like me?"

Rachel smiled. "Mack, you have my blessing."

"Thank you. That means a lot. But, what about her? Is that something she would want?"

"I have some ideas and know her, but that's a direct question for her. I'd advise you to be honest about your recent experience and your feeling. She is independent and makes her own decisions."

"She's just like you," I stated.

Rachael laughed, and said, "Perhaps similar to me in some ways."

I asked, "Is Alena at the gallery?"

"Yes, but why don't you call her first?"

* * *

Rachel gave me Alena's telephone number. With nerves on edge, I went back to my room and called her. She sounded happy to hear my voice and was surprised to learn that I was in Cadaques.

She was busy with the shipment of a painting, so we agreed to meet at seven o'clock, at the same restaurant where we had our last meal together.

Having a couple of hours to kill, I took a shower and once dressed, I looked again around my room and noticed the poetry books on the shelf, particularly the one written by Rachel Eden, *The Mystery of Wisdom*. I took it down and skimmed through the pages. My nerves were on edge because of meeting with Alena, so placed the book back on the shelf. At some point, I would read it in detail.

I left the hotel and walked around Cadaques, remembering the tour that Alena had given me. It was a pleasure to rediscover the small streets and the dark blue sea. It was so different from New York.

In walking past a small fishing boat with a tied-up sail, I dreamed of sailing away. Further on, the sun glistened on the sea, and in the distance, two seagulls flew together triggering memories of a few lines of a poem by Quima Jaume that Alena had quoted.

A flight of juggling gulls
It evokes in us the love of lovers.

I couldn't relax. The expectation of meeting the real Poetic Sea was like balancing my soul on swallows' wings.

* * *

A few minutes before seven, I arrived at the restaurant and chose a table. The evening was cooler than in September but still pleasant. Faint smells from the restaurant's kitchen reminded me that I had skipped lunch. The impassioned songs of Edith Piaf and the other French singers continued to be played over the loudspeakers.

I waited, and suddenly a wave of doubt went through me. What was I doing here? This was unknown territory. Was it right to even think of having a relationship with Alena? We were so different from each other. She was an artist and poet, and I was merely a guy who had mastered a few stock trading methodologies. Whatever happened, I wanted to see her.

At five minutes after seven, Alena walked across the courtyard, tall, confident, with the grace of a ballerina.

I stood, and she smiled and came up to me. I awkwardly stepped toward her, not knowing if it would be a handshake or a hug.

Instead, Alena leaned toward me, and we kissed on each cheek. With a welcoming smile, she said, "Mack, I'm sorry I'm late. It's so good to see you. I've often thought of you."

"You have?" I asked.

"For sure. I've wondered about you."

"It's been a busy time. Please sit. Is this place okay?"

"Of course."

The waiter came and lit the candles on our table, which gave off a soft glow, and I had the impression we entered a world of our own. For our meal, we ordered *Dorade*, a fish from the Mediterranean Sea.

As we waited for the food, Alena said, "Thank you so much for making the introduction to Flo Capelle."

"How is that going? I'm sorry, but I lost track."

"It's progressing very well. Flo asked me to send three paintings, to test the market. She hung them in her gallery, and they all sold in a few days. Flo said she has never seen anything like it. She also sold some of my mother's poem-paintings."

"Amazing," I said. "I'm thrilled. What's the next step?"

"Flo is proposing a formal exhibition in the spring, so I will be working hard through the winter to produce paintings. She wants me to be there at the opening of the exhibition. And, she contacted galleries in Los Angeles and San Francisco."

"Fabulous. When you come to New York, I have guest bedrooms, and you're welcome to stay with me."

She smiled. "That's very kind of you."

Then I thought of my guest bedrooms. Patricia and Jade now occupied two, and I wasn't sure how long they would stay. Honestly, I was glad they could look out for the place, for I wasn't sure I wanted to go back.

The waiter served our meal, grilled fish with slices of lemon and fresh tomatoes.

We ate slowly, enjoying the food and tranquility of the evening, while talking about art, my travels to Africa and Alena's current projects. I mainly listened as Alena described an art exhibit she had visited in Barcelona. I loved the way she brought out the colors and details of the paintings making them vivid with poetic imageries.

When the meal was finished, the waiter cleared the dishes, and instead of having desert, we ordered two glasses of semi-sweet Cava, sparkling wine.

While waiting for Cava, I said, "I was talking to Rachel and asked about you." I didn't know how to put it.

"About me?"

"Every day I look at you."

"What?"

"Your painting is hanging in my living room next to a Jackson Pollock."

"You have a Jackson Pollock?"

"An original."

"Incredible. I'm flattered, but to put my painting next to an abstract expressionist is quite a contrast."

"I know. It doesn't go. Jackson Pollock is moving to another room, maybe the bathroom."

Alena laughed. "You can't do that."

"You're right, and I wouldn't. It will go into my office." We had gone off topic. I said, "Anyway, every day, I look at the painting, and it reminds me of you."

"It is me," she affirmed.

"It's more than looking."

She didn't say anything but patiently waited.

"May I be honest?" I asked.

"It's best."

"I've never been good at relationships, not knowing the protocols. Someone came along, and I got caught up in a dark storm. Now it's finished."

She smiled. "I know."

I was surprised. "How do you know?"

"Flo and I talked a lot about art and galleries, and I asked about you. She told me your story."

"How did she know?"

"It seems that Flo is connected. She already knew about your problems when she went to your apartment to see my painting. Then, she knew about the court hearing. I learned a lot from her, and I felt sad for you. It must have been a tough time."

I took a deep breath. Of course, if anyone would know about Linette and me, it would be Flo. She knew everything that went on in New York, and because I had been a good client, she would have taken an interest in my affairs.

I said, "Yes, it was complicated, and I couldn't release myself. I wasn't free, but now it's different. Life has changed dramatically, and I'm doing things that were unthinkable a couple of months ago."

At that moment the waiter came with the sparkling wine and served it. Light reflected off the sea, through the glasses, adding to the mystical radiance of the evening.

We clinked glasses and sipped the wine and Alena asked, "So, what now?"

Her question was vague and could have been taken in several directions, but by the gentle tone of her voice and exploratory gaze, it was a query leading to something deeper. I took my time and fought through a wall of anxiety wondering how to say it. No matter how it came out, I knew it would be clumsy. "Do you remember the last time we were here, and we danced."

"It was an exquisite evening, never to be forgotten."

"Indeed, it was a special moment. If you remember, you asked if I had ever been in love."

"I remember. It was a cheeky question," Alena stated.

"Cheeky?"

"Mischievous."

"It's a question rarely asked, at least to me. I'm glad you did."

She held her gaze on me and with a soft voice asked, "Your answer was ambiguous. Has something changed?"

"Yes, and some of that change was caused by a painting hanging in my living room. Every day it is a reminder of an extraordinary event in my life, pointing back to the last time we were here. Something happened to me."

She waited for a second, then softly said, "It also stayed with me. It was a wonderful moment, almost like a tipping point, and it left me with wistful memories. We both gained something. You have the painting as a reminder, whereas I remember you every time I walk past this restaurant, which is often."

I looked at her and said, "Seeing your painting and the memory it evokes, I wonder if that enchantment might continue. That's why I'm here." I paused and then with difficulty said, "Is this something you might consider?"

She looked at me, contemplative, not saying anything.

Anxiety rattled through me like a buzz saw. One song ended, and another started over the loudspeakers. I attempted to deflect my awkward declaration and turned the conversation to something else. I asked, "What is that song?"

She glanced at the loudspeakers and then back at me. "It's Edith Piaf singing, *Ne Me Quitte Pas*, written by Jacques Brel. His songs were wonderfully poetic."

"Do you know what it says?"

She answered, "There is much to it, but to roughly translate parts, it says things like,"

Forget the time,
The misunderstandings
And the time that was lost.

And

I will see you
Dancing and smiling
And to listen to you.
Don't leave me.

Alena paused for a moment, her eyes drifting to the loudspeakers and then back to me. She asked, "Was our time here only a memory, or is it to be?"

"It can be both," I said. "Like a hopeful journey."

Alena spoke softly. "A fascinating poet once wrote,"

The space between fingers speaks
To the space between lips
Between letters
Between worlds.

There is nothing sweeter than this distance.

She smiled, stood up, took my hand, and said, "Let's dance." With a firm grip, she pulled me into the open area next to the restaurant tables. She placed us in the proper dancing position, and we began to slowly glide to the music.

Alena leaned in close to me, and whispered, "Mack, you asked if I would consider something, which is, can our special moment continue? On the surface that's a simple question, but underneath, it is like tectonic plates shifting the world."

"I understand that," I said, "but we both need an answer, and I know my desire. It is to be with you. Before, you asked if I have ever been in love. Now, the answer is yes."

She looked me in the eyes and said, "In the painting hanging in your apartment, the girl strolls along the sand with a purpose, quickening toward a mystery she yearns to explore."

I thought of the painting of Poetic Sea, how the young woman moves with resolve in front of a mystical landscape, but like many things Alena said, her words held deeper meanings. I needed clarity and said, "May I ask my question in another way?"

"Of course," she replied.

With nerves on edge, I asked, "Can you and I continue together? To use an illustration, we have both been in separate boats." I nodded toward the boats anchored in the bay. "Is it possible that we might sail in one boat together, forever?" I knew my allegory was simplistic, but Alena thought in those terms.

She stopped moving to the music, and we stood still, looking at each other. With teary eyes, she whispered, "I am overwhelmed with emotion and when searching the deepest part of my being, the answer is found in the title of Jacques Brel's song, *Ne Me Quitte Pas*."

"What does that mean?" I asked.

With a quiet but firm voice she said, "Don't leave me." She gently squeezed my hand.

I reflected for a quick moment, aware of my feelings, knowing what was right, convinced there was only one possible response. With conviction, I resolutely said, "Never."

We swayed as one, as a sweet fragrance emanated from her long brown hair. Her demand had been definitive, a desire that I stay with her. My reply was an iron stake fixed in granite, an everlasting commitment.

Combined with that came a contented realization that my life was going in a new direction. I would not be dictated by fear or what the general culture demanded. Instead, I was tracking footprints that would take us on a unique path, while being led by the One who gives wisdom.

I drifted into a beautiful dream. dancing with Poetic Sea.

Citations

In the beginning of this story, Barry plagiarizes his metaphors. Here, they are cited:

Blue like the sea of a dream. Joseph Conrad
Brown in hue as hazel nuts. William Shakespeare
Red as with wine out of season. Elizabeth Barrett Browning
Heats like the hammered anvil. Oliver Wendell Holmes
Soft as the melody of youthful days. Lord Byron
Hot as a swinked gypsy. Francis Thompson
Confident as Hercules. William Prynne
Strong as the voice of Fate. Edward Bulwer-Lytton
Free as bird on branch, just as ready to fly east as west. Elizabeth Barrett Browning

Barry modified the first lines of Sara Teasdale's poem, I Am Not Yours. Here are Teasdale's original lines:

I am not yours, not lost in you,
Not lost, although I long to be
Lost as a candle lit at noon,
Lost as a snowflake in the sea.

Toward the end of this novel, there is an excerpt from a poem starting with, *The space between fingers speaks.* The poem is titled 'Meanwhile', and is found in the book, 'The Space Between - poems by Anna Elkins'. This is a lovely collection.

Author's Notes

I hope you enjoyed *Poetic Sea*. If you liked it, please leave a comment on the Poetic Sea book page on Amazon.com. Your comments help.

Let me confess upfront that I am a storyteller and not a poet. Having said that, I feel that poetry enriches our experience. Meeting poets is a privilege. Unfortunately, in our Western Culture we have lost this appreciation, and therefore something precious has vanished.

William Wordsworth defined poetry as, "the spontaneous overflow of powerful feelings." Not wanting to disagree with the great master, it seems to me that good poetry goes beyond feelings. As Rachel Eden says, "It is a way of perceiving".

There is a connection between excellent poetry and wisdom. Wisdom is the power of true and just discernment, and that's what good poetry enables. It enlightens and enriches our experience, while touching something profound in our humanness. I'd encourage you to get to know the poets quoted in this book. Also, take a close look at the Book of Proverbs to discover its abundant use of analogies and how it uses them to teach wisdom.

True poets don't just play with words. There is revelation in their works, and there can be elements of truth.

The characters in this novel hold worldviews, or ways of perceiving, and this defines their values and habits. Worldviews get handed to us like pairs of colored glasses. What color is yours? That leads to Rachel Eden's question. Are you living by a culture, or living on the path to wisdom? Where are your footprints leading?

Enjoy,

Cass Tell
www.casstell.com

Other Books by Cass Tell

Cass Tell is the author of numerous novels, short stories and children's books. You can find a complete list of his stories on his website at www.casstell.com.

Here are two recent books for your enjoyment.

A boy discovers that he can see future events. This ability takes him on an extraordinary journey.

Her grandmother's old cookbook contains secret messages. This leads her to a truth that is impossible to face.

Lightning Source UK Ltd.
Milton Keynes UK
UKHW012217140221
378768UK00001B/35